Where the ghosts cry

Stories

by
Judi Moore

*

Illustrated

by
Mat Cross

By the same author

Wonders will never cease
Ice cold passion and other stories
Little Mouse: a novella
Is death really necessary?

Published by Moo Kow Press
in conjunction with FeedARead Publishing

For more information please go to:

www.judimoore.wordpress.com

www.MatCross.net

www.mookowpress.wordpress.com

In these small works of fiction, the characters, places and events are either the product of the author's imagination, or are used in a fictitious context.

Thanks

My grateful thanks to my betareaders from the two creative writing workshops I mention elsewhere – Gary Hawker, Albert Gillen, Val Griffin, Sue Hogben, Babs Kirby, Peter Ruffell, and Kathy Sharp: to Cheri Carroll and Anne Link for their valuable inputs, and to Em King for her vibrant 'Sea Foal' illustration.

Massive thanks to Mat Cross for the illustrations to the other stories, and for the book's cover artwork.

The illustrations (Mat's and Em's) are such an asset to the book. I hope they resonate with readers as happily as they do with me.

Where the gulls cry

short stories set in and
around Weymouth

Contents

Introduction

I came to live in Weymouth in January of 2016.

I grew up in North Cornwall and spent three years on the coast of west Wales, so I'm a country girl at heart. But in order to earn a living I spent 36 years in Milton Keynes. It is the last and best of the new towns, low rise, very green – but oh dear, I did miss the sea.

So I plotted and planned and eventually found the right house in the right town, right on the coast. I've dug in here like a hermit crab in soft sand. I love the light, the art, the music, the natural world, the pink bay at sunset, the lullaby of wavelets on the shingle, the leonine breakers pouncing on the Chesil during a storm.

I've been a professional writer since 1997. So one of the first things I looked for after I'd unpacked pen, paper and computer, was a creative writing workshop. I was lucky enough to find *two* great workshops – Off the Cuff and Weymouth Writing Matters – both of them exercise based. Doing those twenty minute exercises every week, I produced a lot of very short fiction that could only have been made here, in Weymouth.

When Covid closed down our lives in March of 2020 I immediately cast about for a writing project to keep me busy for the duration. There sat 10 notebooks full of workshop exercises, never revisited. I wondered, what's actually in there?

So through lockdown I keyed up the draft

scrawls in those notebooks, unpacking some stories, finishing others, editing and polishing them all.

Nowhere is the pandemic mentioned, because all these tales were told between 2016 and 2019. I'm sure there are many stories to be told about our Covid experiences, but these are not they.

I hope you enjoy them.

Judi Moore
May 2022

Sea Foal

I often walk along the sea front at night. I enjoy the sparkling necklace of lights around Weymouth Bay, and the way the streetlights on Portland isle dither in the constant wind. Out on the island's harbour arms lonely little warning lights wink on and off, red and white. All is peace.

This one evening in early April the most tremendous gale had just blown itself out after rattling the windows for 36 hours. I was stir crazy from all the rain and wind keeping me at home, so decided to go out, and walk myself tired enough to sleep. I tossed a mental coin when I reached the Pier Bandstand, and turned left onto Greenhill Esplanade.

I walked down to where the Preston Wall starts, and sat down for a moment, just to enjoy the night.

The tide was high and on the turn. The moon was full but small and far away, casting long, pale shadows. Little foam-edged waves washed to and fro in the shallows.

*

Further out I could hear splashing. Probably a Bay-swimmer or paddle-boarder returning late, I thought. But then I could hear something else. It was loud, the sort of noise that if you heard it in a dark house you'd quickly be convinced the house was haunted and leave pronto.

The keening continued. It caused the hair to

stand up on the nape of my neck, but I didn't flee. It sounded quite desperate to my ears. Perhaps something was in trouble down by the water, or in it? I hurried down the last few yards onto the beach, and tried to work out where the noise was coming from.

I pulled out my mobile phone and switched it on as I stumbled across the shingle. I'd have light in a minute, when it'd booted up. That should help. I stopped and listened. The phone chirped that it was ready, and I fumbled the flashlight on, shining it up and down the beach and in the shallows.

There?

*

Right up against the groyne, near the high water mark, was a tangle of something which seemed to be moving. Could this be the source of the desperate keening?

The tangle was netting and buoys, snagged on the rocks. It must have been lost from a fishing boat in the gale.

In the middle of the muddle a big dark eye looked up at me.

I caught my breath – it was so unexpected, that eye.

The awful moaning stopped.

I took a step back and played my flashlight over the tangle of net and rope to try and work out what I was looking at. Where was the body to go with the eye? Deep within the tangle it was constantly writhing; was this its body or legs or ... a tail? ... I couldn't see.

I had another look at the head of whatever-it-was. It winced when I shone the light in its eye. I apologised softly for blinding and frightening it. I saw it had a long snout. For a second I thought it was a dog. But then I realised whatever-it-was had no ears.

The creature gaped and gave that dreadful cry of distress again. I saw that the mouth was full of needle-sharp teeth. I was pretty sure it was *something* from the sea. An air breather? A seal? Did they have teeth like that? Or perhaps it was an eel? Did eels scream? If it was an eel I needed to get it back into the sea as quickly as possible.

I sat down beside it and rummaged in my shoulder bag for the Swiss army knife I always carry. I chose the saw blade and started cutting. The creature was still now, watching me with its big dark eye.

When I'd freed a few of the more painful-looking strands of net, a flipper slithered out of the mare's nest. A seal then. Or a seal pup perhaps. It was still difficult to tell what size the animal inside the ball of net was. I kept on sawing at the harsh nylon strands.

I managed to free its tail; at once the creature started writhing like an eel. And it started making that desperate noise again.

I stopped what I was doing and gingerly laid a hand on the little head. It was warm – too warm, I feared. There was no fur there. It felt more like … a slow-worm, perhaps. Sort of dry and slightly scaly.

It didn't shake my hand off or try to bite me. It stopped writhing, but continued gaping and keening. I started talking to it.

'Just lie still for a moment,' I said soothingly. 'Then I can cut you free without hurting you. The more you wriggle the worse tangle you get into. Hush now. Hush.'

It seemed to calm down. I got on with cutting the tough nylon as quickly as I could. I cut myself several times, but I don't believe I cut the ...

*

Suddenly I knew what it was.

The chap who takes people out on The Fleet in his glass-bottomed boat had spoken of it, and pointed out a sculpture of it outside the derelict Ferrybridge Inn. The sculpture, about five feet tall, is of a mythical sea beast, the Veasta, which supposedly lives in the Fleet.

I'd thought it a tall tale for tourists – and certainly the sculpture, of an upright creature very like a seahorse, couldn't possibly exist in the Fleet. It wouldn't have sufficiently powerful fins to swim against the strong currents that wash in and out of the Fleet and Portland harbour. And the Fleet is too shallow for any vertical swimmer of that size to be viable. However, what I was looking at had a head that was definitely horse-like. But its body, now that I could see more of it, was long and sinuous, ending in a powerful tail. It was definitely a horizontal swimmer.

I was looking at something out of legend.

It must've been swept out of the Fleet in the gale, fallen foul of this tangle of fishing gear and been unable to return to its home with the tide.

It fixed me with its big, dark eye and gave a little whimper. It looked exhausted. I began to be afraid it would die before I could free it and redoubled my efforts. Soon my left hand was a mass of cuts and my right was cramped with sawing endless strands of tough nylon. But finally I could see pretty much the whole animal.

It was about the size of a collie dog. It had a pair of powerful front flippers much like a seal, and a muscular tail which still looked more like an eel than anything else. The neck was long – much too long for a seal, as was the head: the whole creature was a streamlined marvel. And obviously a strong swimmer.

Delicately, I picked it out of the remains of its cocoon. It lay limp in my arms.

I carried it down to the sea and laid it at the edge. I didn't want to put it *in* the sea in case it was so far gone it drowned. Its body rocked back and forth in the shallows as the wavelets broke around it, but it made no movements of its own.

Suddenly, about three yards out in the Bay, another Veasta rose out of the water – a much bigger one – and began humping itself through the shallows towards me on its flippers and tail, like a seal. It hissed as it came. It was coming to help its baby.

The little one began to make a weak version of the alarming noise that had first alerted me to

something being wrong on the beach. The mother –
for surely it was she – began to make crooning
noises.

Mother Veasta, standing up on her flippers as
she was now, was as tall as me. I remembered the
array of teeth in the baby's mouth and retreated up
the beach a little way. Her teeth would be much
bigger and she had no reason to think kindly of me.

Mama hauled herself right out of the sea and
began to nudge the little one, rolling it gently into
deeper water. I was sure it was dying. But when a
wavelet broke over it, it seemed to revive a little.
She continued to push it gently out into the Bay.

At that point there was a great commotion off
the end of the groyne. A third Veasta reared up out
of the water and flopped back down with an
almighty crash, like a whale breaching. Presumably
this was how the family's guardian male let
predators know to leave them alone. I shuffled
further back up the beach, picking up my phone and
knife as I went and stuffing them into my (now
soaked) shoulder bag.

It was quite difficult, backing up the beach while
keeping an eye on the family of Veastas, stallion,
mare and foal. The stallion breached several more
times and, finally charged the beach. I stumbled
through the shingle away from him and up onto the
footpath.

The mare continued to coax the foal into deeper
water, keeping it afloat on her neck when it flagged.

I watched from the footpath above the beach
until the little family had swum completely out of

sight.

It wasn't until I got home that I realised I hadn't taken a photograph of what I'd seen. That's why I'm writing it down for you now. But I don't suppose for a moment that you'll believe me.

Sea Foal: "Mother Veasta ... was as tall as me."

Along the Esplanade at night

The moon was hanging low over the sea, a small orange ball, seductively veiled. A most unusual moon. Kit stopped to admire it. Her companion, Toby, sniffed at the base of one of the outsized lamp posts and nonchalantly cocked a back leg.

From the nearby beach huts came a low hum of voices, occasional outbursts of young laughter, and the herby scent of quality skunk.

Kit inhaled and moved on.

*

Holidays were supposed to be fun. Today had been a nightmare. The traffic had been dreadful all the way down, and Trevor even more short-tempered than usual. For the past few months he had been, frankly, unrecognisable as the man she had married and had two children with. The kids, of course, had become fractious. Even Toby – usually the most placid of dogs – had become snappy in the sticky heat of the car, as they crawled along the motorway towards Weymouth, hour after hour.

Trevor had refused to stop more than once, saying that if they got off the motorway they'd never get back on again. Which was, obviously, nonsense – but he couldn't be reasoned with and, to her shame, she hadn't even tried.

And then, after the motorway was finished, the

winding A roads had been just as clogged and progress just as slow, although the familiar, well-loved views from the car had been better.

When they'd finally reached the B & B and unloaded the car, everyone had had a pee, a wash and combed their hair, then she'd insisted they go straight out to eat. The kids were hungry, but they were also very tired and she wanted to get some food inside them before they started acting up or dozing off. Trevor had wanted a drink first. They had compromised by looking for somewhere they could sit down which had a licence. But the kids hadn't like the look of most of those menus. And several wouldn't allow dogs in. So that became fraught too.

Eventually they found somewhere that was family and dog friendly and where Trevor could have a pint. She felt the need of a glass of wine herself. She'd have one later, after the kids were asleep. Maybe more than one.

*

The kids, their little bellies now full of chips, were asleep on their feet on the way back. Fern's little feet started to drag. Trevor said they'd get where they were going quicker if he carried her. But she complained about his beer breath so he put her down again and made her walk. She began to grizzle. Robin marched bravely on, but he was wandering from side to side, and then started to lag behind. She took hold of his hand and tugged him along. She knew he wouldn't want to be carried like a baby. Robin was getting to be a big boy now.

*

When they got back to the guesthouse, Fern and
Robin flopped into bed like rag dolls, clothes still on,
teeth uncleaned, faces unwashed. Trevor wanted
to wake them up and get them properly ready for
bed, but Kit said,

'Leave them. They're tired out.'

'What about me? I'm tired out. I don't go to bed
in my clothes!'

He wanted a row, she could see it in his eyes.
She said,

'there's a bottle of wine in the cooler bag. Have
yourself a glass or two. Leave me some.'

'Where the fuck are you going?'

'I'm going to walk Toby. I need some air.'

Trevor's mouth opened to say something
unpleasant, but she was out of the room before he
could articulate whatever it was. She was
determined not to rise to his barbs. And whatever
insult he'd been working up to, if she hadn't heard it
she didn't have to think what to do about it. But all
the same she felt the tears pricking the back of her
eyes again.

They'd been to Weymouth every year since
Robin was born, and it was always the same. They'd
drive down with Trevor for some reason feeling put
upon, and barely controlling a simmering rage.
There'd be a row (in hissed undertones) the night
they arrived. Then, if it didn't rain, they would have
a nice week on the beach until the day before they

went home, when there would be another row which would last all the way home. They could put up with each other all year, it seemed – until they came away on holiday.

Sometimes she wondered why they bothered coming.

*

It was a humid night. There was almost as much water in the air as there was washing softly up and down the beach. It was a challenge to push through the heavy air, one foot after the other. She stopped again. There was always lots to see at night on the Esplanade. Over the railings, down on the beach, a number of castle-building projects of greater and lesser complexity were crumbling under the creeping onslaught of the tide. Those turrets and moats stood proudly until the wavelets reached them, or until the council tractor raked them flat sometime around dawn, ready for the next day's builders.

Over all, gulls swooped like ghosts, or squabbled like banshees over discarded chips. Even a gull must eat, she thought, moving on again.

Here was Madame Aurora's gaily painted booth. "Let Madame Aurora read your palm" read one of the panels on the gypsy's kiosk. Another said "Madame Aurora can help and advise". If only visiting a fortune teller could do the trick, Kit thought. Toby trotted on to the next lamp post. She followed him.

Above them, the lamp began to wink on and off.

Was it random, or some complicated pattern?

It was hard not to imagine that it knew something she didn't; that it was sending a message. She wished she understood what it was trying to tell her. But then, that was always the problem, wasn't it?

Her mum had always maintained that Kit expected too much from her man.

'Your shared task is the children,' said her mum. 'Apart from that, keep your own counsel, earn your own money, live your own life, and don't rely on him for everything.'

This was so alien to the modern idea of romantic soul mates sharing everything, that Kit had been astonished.

'But you and dad have a wonderful marriage!'

'That's why. We don't get under each other's feet. We aren't joined at the hip like you and Trevor. Your dad does what he wants and I do what I do. You need to keep some distance.

'Just think about how it feels to be able to go into the bathroom and lock the door for half an hour.'

Kit had snorted with laughter at that.

'I haven't been able to do that since Robin was born!'

'Exactly,' said her mother.

So how would her mother approach a week in Weymouth? If they didn't usually spend their weeks in each others' pockets, then a week away, with quality time for each other, would be romantic – even with the children. It could be a time to rekindle what had brought them together in the first place. Possibly easier on a Greek island, but perfectly possible in Weymouth.

Trevor wasn't as gorgeous as he had been when they met. Less hair. More belly. But then, her gorgeousness quotient had dropped too. She hardly ever bought any new clothes. It was just too difficult, having to take Robin and Fern with her to the shops. Perhaps she should take a long hard look at herself. She had a suspicion she wasn't Kit any more – she was "mum".

She reeled in Toby's lead and turned in the direction of the B & B. Hopefully, there would be a glass of wine left for her. Trevor might still be awake. Although he had had a long day's driving. Why did he do all the driving, anyway? She was a perfectly good driver. They could easily have shared the drive. He let her drive when they went out, so he could have a drink. She realised suddenly the ramifications of that word 'let': and was hit with a sudden suspicion that he did all the 'family driving' because he didn't want to have to deal with amusing the children in the car.

'Some things are going to have to change,' she told Toby as they walked back. 'Starting this week.'

There was a spring in her step now that hadn't been there when she set out.

Indeed, it hadn't been there for some time.

Along the Esplanade at night: "Above them, the lamp began to wink on and off."

The broken locket

It had been one of those Bank Holidays which breaks records: a glorious blue-sky Boxing Day. The whole population had apparently cancelled whatever plans they had made for the rest of the Christmas holiday and headed for the coast. Weymouth beach, which had been sparsely populated by well-muffled dog walkers on an overcast Christmas Day, was almost invisible under the throng. Some people made summer-style encampments. Children were working hard with buckets and spades. There were people in the water!

But this was nearly the shortest day of the year. The sun sank early, the day grew cold. When the sun left the beach the swarm of day-trippers departed as one. Behind them they left bins overflowing with trash – and rich pickings for metal detectorists.

*

Will wasn't the only detectorist hurrying down onto the sand. He was keen to beat his rivals and the incoming tide to the gold and silver he knew would lie just under the much-scuffed surface of the beach.

Up and down the beach others with metal detector equipment were stepping out onto the sands. He knew most of them – Sandy, Tom, Ian, the Polish couple from Poole, several others he knew by sight – and they had established their own little territories over time.

Will's patch was around the slipway behind the town clock at the top of King's Street. A lot of footfall went through there, as people walked to and from the Swannery car park. The sun was going down and already the light was fading, but he'd brought a head torch, for later. He got to work right away.

After half an hour he had a handful of gold rings, a couple of less valuable dress rings, a few broken gold and silver chains, and a locket. It was a particularly pretty, gold locket that looked old. He'd had to dig quite deep for this one, and he wasn't at all sure it had been dropped today. He wondered, idly, how long it had taken for it to sink down that far into the sand.

*

Straightening up to ease his back, he looked out to sea for a moment. A sea mist was rolling in. Then he became aware of someone coming towards him down the slipway. It was a girl, wearing a Forties-style vintage dress in an ethereal shade of blue that almost merged with the twilight. She'd done her hair up in those big rolls girls sometimes wore in World War II movies. She seemed dressed for a party. From his own teenagers, Will was well aware that fashion trumped air temperature every time. But he wondered how come this girl had no coat. It was getting really cold now. His nose and ears were chilled.

The girl was making straight for him. She was so graceful she seemed to be floating. She was certainly going against the flow. She must have forgotten something on the sand. Or lost something.

Standing still, Will felt gooseflesh start on his arms and the back of his neck. That was the trouble with detecting: first you got hot, then cold, then hot – and so it went.

The girl walked right up to him. She didn't waste any time with pleasantries. She said,

'You've found my locket.'

It wasn't a question.

'I suppose I may have done. D'you know where you lost it?'

It must be the gold locket that she meant. That was worth good money if he was any judge. Which he was. He'd be due a finder's fee anyway. It was gratifying to reunite someone with a treasured piece of jewellery. It saved him having to sell it on for the scrap gold or silver price. But he had discovered that the trick was to get recompense for his efforts before handing over the item. He'd had cards printed for just this purpose. He fingered them in his pocket.

'It broke.'

'Can you describe it?' He wasn't about to let her paw through his little haul and pick out the locket without more information than that.

'It's gold. Chased.'

The antique locket was chased. It might be hers.

'D'you want to have a look at what I've found,'

he held out the handful of finds, 'see if it's here?'

She picked through them delicately with a forefinger and quickly pounced on the broken gold locket.

'This,' she said, and clasped it in her fist. She brought the fist to her mouth and kissed it.

That she was now holding the locket at once reduced the likelihood that Will could get it back, or a finder's fee out of her. Nevertheless, he tried,

'You could give me something for finding it for you,' he ventured.

'Oh, I couldn't do that,' she said.

Will bristled a bit.

'Well, you wouldn't have found it without me!' he said.

'I came back for it specially. I knew you'd found it.'

This was getting a bit weird. He looked up at the Esplanade, above them at the top of the slipway. Where could she have been standing to see him find it? And how could she possibly have known it was hers?

She went on,

'They were shipping out. It was all very sudden. There was a Farewell Ball at the Royal Hotel. I wore my new dress.' She picked at the skirt of her blue frock with the fingers of the hand not clutching the locket. 'We came out here to get some air. I thought he was going to propose, but he didn't. Instead he got this locket out of his pocket and offered it to me, just like that, in his hand. He said it was his mother's. I thought he'd probably picked it up cheap in a pawnshop. I let him put it round my neck, although I was so disappointed. Then he tried to kiss me and I wouldn't let him.' There were tears in her eyes now. 'He asked me to wait for him, and I said I wouldn't. My mother always said never to trust a soldier – nor a sailor neither for that matter. When you're out of sight you're out of mind, my mother always said. And I'd met a nice local boy who worked on his father's farm at Osmington. That was a proper job too, feeding the country, and no endless waiting around for him to come back from some unpronounceable place.

'So he wanted the locket back, and I wouldn't give it to him. We fought, and somehow it came off. We spent ages looking for it, but we couldn't find it. Then he stormed off and left me here. It was the worst night of my life.'

Will felt they'd stepped outside of time, somehow. Her story had him spellbound, but puzzled. He felt it might all come clear yet, but he needed to know more.

'So why are you so keen to have the locket back?'

She looked out to sea when she said. 'Because he never came back.'

'Were you expecting him to?'

'Oh. I wasn't expecting him to come back to *me* after I'd been so mean to him. But everyone expected that the *regiment* would come home. Only it didn't. The ship they were travelling on sank. They never even arrived where they were going.

'He's still out there somewhere, in the water. It's preyed on my mind, to be honest. I'd like to return it to him. Only I could never find it. And now you have.' She turned to him smiling, her face now wet with tears. 'Thank you.'

She turned away from him with a swirl of blue, the locket still held tight in her fist. It was really cold on the beach now. And so dark it was getting hard to see. He switched on his head torch. The beach leapt into focus. But the girl was gone.

The broken locket: 'She was so graceful she seemed to be floating.'

Mirage or miracle

It was 33°centigrade according to Harry's iphone.

It was so hot that all we could contemplate was sitting quietly, not touching, at either end of the sofa watching box sets, with the windows open as wide as they would go, the curtains drawn, and both fans on. It was too hot for icecream – it became lukewarm custard before you had chance to eat it. Strawberries went from deliciously ripe to rotten before you got a chance to add sugar and cream.

The hours dragged by.

By the time the sun went down, we had binge-watched the whole of the first season of "Game of Thrones". That world sure does have long winters. How we envied them all that lovely ice and snow. It made us feel cooller ourselves. For about five minutes.

Finally, about nine in the evening, it was cool enough for us to move. We put on sandals and our loosest lightest clothes, and emerged blinking, sneezing and snuffling into the August twilight like a couple of ancient asthmatic hedgehogs. Heat sure does tire you out. Wearily we strolled along the Esplanade, beside the high tide, seeking a breeze.

Harry said,

'How about a swim?'

'Nah,' I said. 'We didn't bring our swim togs. And the beach is still busy.'

'I could go back for them,' Harry offered,

heroically.

'Nah.' It was too hot to make decisions like that. Or to take exercise, even in cool water. We had been completely drained of energy by the heat.

He let it lie after that.

*

Tasty cooking smells were coming from the hotels, restaurants, cafés, takeaways and pubs along the Esplanade. They reminded us that we hadn't eaten all day. Harry remained in valiant mode,

'I don't mind cooking,' he said.

'You're surely not contemplating switching on any part of the stove?' I protested. 'And, anyway, there's nothing in the house to cook. We haven't shopped.'

'Nor we have,' he agreed. 'So it's pub or takeaway. You choose.'

My mouth opened to do so when a mechanical rendition of "Jingle Bells" blared out.

'Where's that coming from?' said Harry.

We turned on the spot, seeking the origin of what I hesitate to call music.

*

Shortly the source hove into view, trundling slowly towards us – an old V-Dub van, refurbished as a mobile caff. On the sides, front and back was daubed "Sam's Red-Hot Sizzlers. I sweat so you don't have to."

'It's a mirage,' said Harry.

'It's a miracle,' said I. 'We don't even have to walk

to the chippy now.'

We bellied up to the serving hatch.

'What have you got?' Harry asked.

'Whatever you want.' Said a jolly, perspiring chap clad in white and brandishing a fish slice – presumably Sam.

I ordered spicy chicken fajitas. Harry wanted a vindaloo ('might as well – the theory is you feel cooler, after'). Sam produced both with a flourish of his fish slice. I have no idea how he could possibly offer such a wide menu in that tiny space. I didn't hear the giveaway ping of a microwave. Somewhere in the van there must've been an assistant, conjuring up meals. But where such a person could possibly have been stashed ...

Our minds couldn't even begin to unravel that mystery in our current condition.

*

We collected our food and went and sat on the wall between the beach and the Esplanade to eat it.

Everything was delicious.

Sam got back in the driving seat of his V-Dub, switched "Jingle Bells" on again, and continued up the Esplanade.

About a hundred yards away from us, an almighty bang came from the back of the microbus, and it was enveloped in a cloud of remarkably sweet-smelling smoke. More like barbeque than blown engine.

'Should we go and help him?' I asked Harry.

Harry – still glassy-eyed from the vindaloo –

shook his head. 'I don't think Sam ever really had all four wheels in our reality. He was a sort of figment, a wish fulfilment.' He smiled. 'Although I can still taste that vindaloo.'

'I suspect you'll still be able to do that tomorrow morning.'

Mirage or miracle: 'he was a sort of figment ...'

The Fortune-teller's Summer

On the Esplanade here, opposite one of the nicer hotels, there is a little five-sided kiosk. Beside the door is a sign, on which is written, in golden gothic lettering: *let Madame Aurora tell your fortune. Marriages fixed. Unborn babies sexed. Wayward spouses hexed. Careers progrexxed.*

*

Madame Aurora returns to this kiosk every year, just in time for the second spring Bank Holiday. On arrival, she renews the glamour that she set over it when she first moved in years before (to save repainting), and the spell which disguises it from the local council (which would otherwise certainly want her to pay a substantial rent for it).

Madame Aurora does not do things by halves. When she moves in each spring she moves *everything* in: her comfy lounge with its squashy three piece suite and 50 inch TV; her well-appointed kitchen, with its granite worktops and range cooker; her bathroom, complete with jacuzzi bath; her bedroom, with its four-poster bed and silk drapes; her back porch, with its relaxing hammock and, beyond, a nice outdoor space for her two Jack Russells. It's a tight fit in a kiosk five feet in diameter, but Aurora is a sorceress of both power and determination.

Having completed her conjuring she relaxes in her hammock on the back porch with a large vodka cranberry. She muses, as she surveys her accomplishments, on the night of passion she once enjoyed with her fellow Polish émigré, the long departed Pietr Brachacki, first set designer for Doctor Who. She had let slip far too many of her secrets that night under the influence of a particularly potent Pan Galactic Gargleblaster (oh yes, they do exist) and the result was Pietr immortalised her kiosk for the BBC no less (and on an appropriately tiny BBC budget).

*

One morning Aurora is sitting outside her kiosk, polishing her crystal ball, when she hears a Maserati growl along the Esplanade. Could this be her summer fling arriving, she asks herself.

Aurora is a bit of a petrolhead – the throaty roar of eight valves really gets her juices flowing – so she cranes her neck to get a better look at the car. What she sees makes her drop her crystal ball in confusion, in the process accidentally covering the palm trees on the Prom in purple candy floss, and creating a watch of very alarmed nightingales which burst into existence singing for help at the tops of their little lungs. By the time Aurora has fixed all that, the sexy Maserati has disappeared.

But the summoning of a sorceress must be obeyed: Aurora calls and the car quickly reappears. With a screech of tyres, it pulls into a parking space which magically appears outside the hotel opposite, and a handsome man gets out looking puzzled.

*

Aurora is on him in a flash, at the same time working her clever, magical fingers behind her back, to fashion some genuine(ish) Dürer etchings for her boudoir.

She whisks the handsome man into her kiosk so briskly that the 'closed' sign is still revolving when the door shuts behind him.

He says, "Wha ...?"

She places an immaculately manicured forefinger on his lips.

He says, "How ...?"

She says, "I heard you coming." Then, after a little more spell-casting behind her back she adds, "See! I've made you a meal. All your favourites!"

But food spells should never be rushed like that. So, the romantic meal is a puzzle too: the Beef Wellington is stuffed with apricots and the sweet crumble contains a juicy tenderloin.

But who needs food, when love is in the air?

"Tell me your name?" She pleads, tugging him in the direction of her boudoir and the four-poster bed with silken hangings.

"B-B-Billy," he stammers.

"Come to my bower, my darling Billy," she insists. And he is putty in her hands.

*

For a week the fortune-teller's kiosk remains closed – which is odd in high season – while Aurora

and Billy her Maserati Man love and eat and drink
and love and talk and love and take long drives in
his car with the top down and the wind in their hair.

*

But on the eighth day Aurora notices a
policewoman taking down the registration number
of her lover's beautiful car (still occupying its
magical space outside the hotel).

As casually as possible, Aurora drifts across the
road and enquires,

'Does anything appear to be the matter, officer?'

'As a matter of fact, the owner of this car has
been reported missing. I don't suppose you've
noticed how long this car has been parked here?'

Although she pleads ignorance, Aurora knows
her time is up. It is time to undo the spells, lift the
wards and let Billy and his Maserati go.

Thus ends Aurora's Whitsun fling, as she sends
her dazed and exhausted lover back to the bosom
of his family.

Of course, the sun is always shining somewhere
on Aurora's annual sun-worshipping migration. She
has many other seaside kiosks; there will be other
V8 sports cars – even some straight sixes – passing
by those kiosks with a throaty roar, being driven by
other handsome Billys. And, hopefully, her magical
meal preparation will improve as the year wears on.

The fortune-teller's summer: 'the summoning of a sorceress must be obeyed ...'

Living with Lady Blackwood

We'd always wanted to live by the sea. Nick hated his job, and I didn't want the shift work any more; so when the kids were off our hands we decided to give up working for other people, buy ourselves a guesthouse in Weymouth and work for ourselves.

What we ended up with was a five storey leasehold Georgian property that had a life story considerably more impressive than anywhere else we had lived. It was certainly more impressive than our own.

But nowhere in any of the documentation, the search, the survey, or the otherwise useful document the previous lessees had prepared and left for us, was there any mention of the ghost.

*

Neither of us believed in ghosts. But you can't argue with a lady dressed head to toe in Victorian mourning (complete with heavy veil) who floats up and down six flights of stairs wringing her hands and moaning softly. It is not a prank. It is not a trick of the light. It is not too much cheese for supper.

The first time I saw her I was as close to her as I am to you now. She isn't scary, exactly. Neither is she solid; she's more a waft of emotion, stuck in the house, unable to get out, or away, or forwards, or even backwards. She has unfinished business in

Gull House, I think it's fair to say.

The first time we saw her we had men up on scaffolding, attending to the roof. Fifteen minutes after she appeared to us indoors, while we were still in a state of shock, one of the workmen fell off the scaffolding outside. What a dreadful thing to happen! We called the ambulance, which came in minutes. But the poor man died on the way to hospital.

The next time we saw 'our ghost', my mother had a bad stroke and was dead two days later. She was 160 miles away at the time. So there was no way she had been frightened to death by our veiled apparition. But it was a second death foretold all the same.

The third time we saw the veiled lady, Nick got an email from an ex-colleague to say that his old boss had died unexpectedly. A septic belly button, apparently.

We began to perceive a pattern.

*

I looked up our ghost online. Something I should, perhaps, have done at the outset of our relationship with her.

The story of Lady Blackwood was easy enough to find.

She had been holidaying in our guesthouse with her four children in 1889. One day, they had all gone to the beach. The nanny had the morning off, so Lady Blackwood was watching them herself. Her little girl had run down to the edge of the sea to fetch a bucketful of water to test the moat the three boys were digging. There she trod on a Portuguese Man O' War jellyfish and quickly became seriously ill. Lady Blackwood organised a swift return to the guesthouse and got the proprietor to send for a doctor. But the poison was all round the poor little girl's body by the time anything sensible could be done. The toddler died that evening.

Lady Blackwood had been up and down the stairs all day, first checking to see if the doctor had been sent for, then to check he was on his way, later asking for hot water and towels to try and draw the poison, finally for cold compresses to try and bring down the child's fever.

'Oh, crap,' said Nick. 'We'll have to give up the lease and start again.'

'Rubbish,' I said. 'People have been running a guesthouse here before, during and since Lady Blackwood holidayed here. Proprietors have been coping with her for over a hundred years. She doesn't *cause* death – she merely gives early warning.'

'Something our predecessors here might have given us,' Nick observed caustically.

'True enough. But that would have been an interesting addendum to "things you might find useful to know" I'm not sure how I would've phrased it, are you?'

I just hope she leaves the paying guests out of it,' said Nick. 'And by the way – she's standing right behind you.'

Living with Lady Blackwood: 'Her little girl had run down to the edge of the sea ...'

A girl called Ocean

I like to come to Weymouth in the summer. It's warm. It's easier being homeless where it's warm. And I like the coast. If someone said to me 'you can be homeless on this Greek island', pfft – I'd take it in a heartbeat. But Weymouth'll do.

Weymouth has some little night clubs along the Esplanade. I've never been into any of them. But I often sit in the pretty Victorian shelter across the road for a while in the evening. The clubs have good live music most nights.

While I'm listening I sometimes meet interesting people. Like this girl who called herself Ocean.

*

She walked out of the 'Lazy Lizard' one evening and crossed the road to the beach. She attracted my attention right away. There was just something about her.

She leaned on the rail between the beach and the prom for a while, waiting for someone perhaps. Then she took off her shoes and went down the steps onto the beach.

She started dancing on the sand to the music floating across the road from the club. She was definitely waiting for someone. The dancing wasn't really for her. Not just for her, anyway.

Then I thought, what if she's waiting for me? It could happen. She might not even realise it was me she was waiting for. She might not have anyone

47

specific in mind. She might be looking for adventure. I could be an adventure. I could be cleaner and not carrying my home around with me, and have drunk fewer cans of White Lightning. But none of that meant I couldn't be some girl's adventure for the evening. I'm not a bad person.

You have to think like this when you live the way I do. We all have our little ways to keep The Dream alive. Mine is super-strong cider, with some it's ganja, with others it's uppers or downers. Then there are the fubars: the meth-heads always on an urgent mish for the next hit; the heroin addicts having the best time of their lives inside their own heads – *living* The Dream, you might say – while their abandoned bodies get sicker until they die.

Sorry. Didn't mean to get heavy there. I see it all, living rough. Some of it makes my heart bleed, truly. But the only person you can help, when you're in this situation, is yourself. So I see it all and say nothing. Until something tickles it with a feather and it all comes spewing out. Like now.

*

So. This girl.

I went down onto the beach and hung around near her. Not near enough to be weird, but just so she'd know I was there. I made sure to keep moving (not getting closer to her, just up and down, pretending to scavenge the top of the beach).

The tide was way out, so far you couldn't see the sea. She was drawing flowers in the wet sand with her hands – great big daisies and roses and lilies.

She had real talent. I went a little bit closer just so as to see them properly, and said,

'They're lovely, those flowers.'

She said,

'Thanks.'

I knew as soon as she spoke that I wasn't the one she was waiting for. But we got chatting anyway. That's how I found out she was called Ocean – although I bet that's not what's on her birth certificate. I began to see she was a work in progress. Even a reconstruction, perhaps.

I wondered what she'd been before.

I've been reconstructed and deconstructed myself a few times over the years. It may scare you a little to learn that most people are only three life crises away from sleeping rough. You *should* be a little scared because, trust me, those sorts of crises frequently come in threes. You lose your job; you get into debt; you lose your home: boom! There you are, scrabbling about at the bottom of the pile, still reeling, wondering what the fuck just happened. There are a bunch of other things you can lose too, when you lose your grip on life; self-respect, wife, children, health …

I spend my days now cadging food and begging for money to buy my drink and smoke, and my nights getting moved on or pissed on. It's OK in the summer, most of the time. But the winter … Sometimes I think I ought to try reconstructing myself again. But it's a long way back up there, bootstrapping, from where I am now.

I couldn't get to sleep that night. The wind switched around to the east after I'd made my pitch and blew in cold over me. Rather than lie there and get a stiff neck, about half past two I thought I'd get a jump start on breakfast, and mished over to Domino's. Sometimes, if it's near closing time, they'll let you have a stale pizza they can't sell.

And there was Ocean. She'd found the person she was waiting on the beach for. They were rowing, not a polite, hissed row with carping and sarcasm (my ex used to do a good line in those), but a full-blown screaming match with arm waving and foot stamping, the works.

They got asked to leave: escorted out. But Domino's aren't stupid – they made them a pizza first, and took the money.

On their way out she threw the pizza box at him.

After they'd gone (still fighting) I grabbed up the box of pizza quick. It was fresh and hot, like her.

I hadn't had anything as good for a long time.

A girl called Ocean: 'It's easier being homeless where it's warm.'

What lies beneath

Brandon, Freddie, my sister Emily and me (I'm Andy, by the way – pleased to meet you) have been coming to Weymouth since we were little kids. In those early years we'd all cram into a static caravan overlooking the Fleet. Now we're grown ups and we bring ourselves. The last couple of years, now we've got steady relationships and jobs (some of us one, some the other, Freddie has both), we've gone all sophisticated and we take an air B & B with a view of the Bay. I mention all this to show you we've got history with this town. We know it well. Or we thought we did.

*

On our first morning we schlepped our gear down to the beach and set up with the Esplanade at our backs. We were there early enough to get a good pitch. Except that we were behind a small dune of sand. We didn't think anything of it to begin with. But as the morning wore on we noticed that it interfered with our view of the sea and the Punch and Judy Show. Brandon's girl, Dee, didn't care. She can spend all day laid on a lounger that one. All you have to do for her is turn her and baste her every so often, hand her a fresh beer from time to time and fetch her a burger at lunchtime. She comes on holiday with a bag full of novels, brings a different one down to the beach every day. I reckon she'll read the lot the fortnight we're here. Loves it she does.

But Brandon, Freddie and I aren't very good at lying on a beach *per se*. Carol (Freddie's partner) and my sis Emily get a bit antzy after an hour or so too.

The day rather stretched out before us. What to do, what to do?

And that pile of sand was really beginning to rankle with me.

The day was already beginning to pall.

Now we've been staring at this sand mound for maybe an hour. I'm wishing now that we'd set up camp somewhere else. Actually, I'm feeling a bit claustrophobic, stuck here behind something the size of a whale. I say as much to Brandon.

'I know,' says Brandon, 'let's build a sandcastle. A proper, champion sandcastle. If we build it off to the right, over here, using this bloody great dune in front of us, we'll improve our view as well. So when we've finished, and we're kicking back with our well-earned beers. We shall be kings of all we survey.'

'And queens,' Carol put in.

'Queens, too,' said Brandon, laughing. 'I'll drink to that.'

So we left Dee in charge of the camp and went in search of implements.

*

We cleaned the nearby beach shops out of decent sand spades, and got one of every kind of bucket available, so as to have a good variety of turrets.

53

When we got back to Dee, we felt the need of a libation to set us up for the project ahead, so we raided the cooler bag. While we partook we tried to apportion the equipment. This led to an argument as to who should get what.

Finally everybody had something. Or did they? Who was missing? Freddie.

Turned out, he'd just picked up a spade and started digging. By the time we'd divvied up the rest of the spades he was standing at the bottom of a substantial pit, tapping his spade on something just under the sand.

'Look,' he said.

We looked.

'It's a manhole cover,' he said.

Under a beach seemed an odd place to find a manhole cover. But the beach changes every year: the sand moves. Sometimes it piles up against the Esplanade, sometimes it gets washed right out into the bay. Sometimes the council retrieves it from the bay with dredgers and dumps it back where it came from. You can see from the steps down to the beach that the level of the sand used to be a lot lower once: the handrails are half-buried.

This manhole cover might have stood level with the beach at some point in its past. We weren't so familiar with the town beach that we could remember if we'd ever seen manhole covers on it (or in it). But we had certainly found one.

We were intrigued. They might've been a feature of the beach once. People might've used them as picnic tables in years gone by. Beach-battles might've been fought over them. There might, indeed, be others up and down the beach, lurking beneath the sand. The town stood right at sea level; perhaps this was something to do with drains. Sewers, even.

We peered down into Freddie's hole. He was clearing off the manhole cover with obvious pride.

It was wider than my shoulders, sitting on a concrete plinth, hinged on one side.

'There's a padlock,' said Emily. She obviously thought we should leave it alone.

Freddie nudged it inquisitively with his spade. It fell open.

'Well, we might as well see what's down there,' said Brandon.

*

We circled the windbreaks to give ourselves extra privacy and levered the iron cover up, with some difficulty.

Two of our better beach spades soon gave way under the strain, but the harder it was to do, the more we wanted to do it.

We had a break for further refreshments, and resumed.

Finally we were able to pull the cover up enough to get a waft of stale air from the hole.

We cheered. Our cheer attracted some attention from neighbouring sunworshippers. Emily shushed us.

'Great. We've done it! Now drop it back,' Emily said.

But Brandon demurred.

'After all that effort, let's see what's down there first,' he said, fishing his mobile out of his back pack.

He placed his feet on either side of the open manhole and took the strain of the half-open cover on his back. Carol and Freddie lay on the sand on the side of the manhole cover's hinge.

'Altogether!' he grunted, and straightened his knees. Carol and Freddie pulled on the sides of the cover.

Between the three of them they quickly had it up and over the vertical. Now it lay flopped over one of the windbreaks like it needed a little lie-down.

People were going to want to know what was going on soon. I suspected what we were doing was at least mildly illegal. But now I wanted to know what was down there as badly as Brandon did.

*

Brandon disappeared into the manhole. Carol, Freddie and I were peering into the hole. Dee had moved her lounger back into the sun, outside our digging perimeter and was engrossed in her book. Emily was trying very hard to pretend that she had no connection to our current enterprise. Carol called down to Brandon,

'What can you see?' Emily shushed her.

Brandon's hollow voice floated up,

'There's a tunnel. It runs both ways, up under the Esplanade and down towards the sea. It doesn't smell too bad now it's aired out a bit. I don't think it's a sewer.'

Carol said to those of us still above ground,

'You wouldn't have a sewer emptying untreated waste into the sea. Not these days.'

'Oh, I don't know,' said Emily. 'It's a pretty old-fashioned place.'

'No,' I said. 'There are laws. I'm pretty sure. You can't just flush turds straight into the sea any more.'

Emily shrugged. She said,

'What *is* it for then?'

'I have no idea,' I said.

'Exactly, said Brandon, emerging, mole-like, from the hole. 'Let's go and have a look.'

Saying which, he turned on his mobile phone's flashlight, hunkered back down into the tunnel and set off. We looked at each other, got out our own phones and, one after another, scrambled into the tunnel after him.

*

So now we were crawling along, like gnomes, with our knees banging on our chins, in a dank and claustrophobic little tunnel.

Back on the beach, in the pleasant sunny day we had left behind, a contretemps was faintly audible. I could hear Emily becoming high-pitched. Never a good sign.

Then, without warning, there was an almighty "clang" and the manhole cover crashed back into place.

'Bugger,' said Freddie. 'Didn't see that coming.'

We swivelled around as well as we could in the extremely confined space and chin-walked our way back to where we'd come in. I was at the front now (there was no room to change places in our single-file scenario). At least when we arrived at the vertical shaft we could all stand upright again. And what a cosy experience that was, the four of us in a space very little bigger than the manhole cover which had started this whole fubar, all waving our flashlights around and blinding each other.

I played my flashlight over the manhole cover above us. What was I expecting to see? I don't know. A chink of light would've been good. The access tunnel were at the bottom of wasn't much to look at. The manhole cover was about ten feet above us. Fixed to the wall inside it and hanging part-way beneath it, was a rusty bit of iron ladder which we hadn't paid nearly enough attention to on our way in.

I was beginning to sober up. I remembered now that I was claustrophobic. It was the teeny tiny tunnel, stretching darkly away from us on either hand, which reminded me. As a fun way to work up an appetite for lunch, exploring this tunnel had really begun to pall. I remembered now what a very bad idea beer before lunch usually was. I was itching to get back to the sun, sand and more beer which which awaited us on the beach above. I'd been at the back of the gnome-walkers until just now. Why the hell hadn't I dropped off the back of the procession? I doubt they'd've missed me. I wasn't essential to the excursion. But now our way out had slammed shut. Damn! That rusty ladder began higher up than I remembered coming down.

But I was seriously motivated to investigate the now-closed manhole cover with a view to rendering it not-closed. Somebody would have to give me a boost up as far as the iron ladder so I could climb back up and try and get the cover open. Then we would have to hope the ladder held long enough for us all to climb out.

*

I opened my mouth to say all this, when I heard an ominous clanking noise travelling up the pipeline towards us from the seaward side. My claustrophobia pricked up its ears.

'What the ...?' I exclaimed. I inhaled. 'Smell that!' I added, as an overpowering smell of seawater hit us. I ducked out of the vertical shaft and shone my flashlight seawards. Sure enough a forefoot of busy black water, with a sweet little frothy wave on top of it, was working its way towards us like an over-friendly puppy, making snuffly noises as it came.

I thought we were going to be under water any moment, and abandoned all thoughts of somehow climbing out of the tunnel the same we we'd got in.

'It must be the tide,' said Brandon. 'It's coming in.'

'Tides do that,' said Carol. 'Twice a day. Whether you're ready for them or not.'

This was my fear. I said,

'We should get out of the tunnel!' As I spoke I

could see Freddie playing his flashlight over that friendly pup of an incoming tide, now licking at our sandals and trainers.

'How full do you think this pipe gets?' said Carol with a touch of panic in her voice. 'Do you think we can get the cover open in time?'

'Or,' said Freddie, 'do you think we can all hang on to the ladder until the tide goes down again?'

'No,' Carol, Brandon and I chorused.

There was a short silence, broken only by the merry gurgling of incoming sea water.

'If it's all the same to you guys, I'd rather not die down here,' I said. The remark was supposed to come out offhand and ironic, but came out sounding quavery and full of fear. I was, after all, now standing in water with an appreciable current tickling my ankles.

'This way,' shouted Freddie. He ducked down again to adopt our previous method of travel and, sensibly, set off in the direction away from the water – which was definitely moving faster now: really rocking up the pipe behind us.

Walking crabbed over like this made progress pretty slow. For some reason I was at the back again; nearest the water, just the place to put your hysterical, claustrophobic friend.

And they were getting ahead of me.

Up ahead, Freddie let out a whoop.

'There are some steps here. And I think there's another hatch. Quick!'

I didn't need encouragement: I was already going as fast as I could. The incoming tide had caught me up and was now threatening to tip me over. It had passed my feet without so much as a "hello, how are you", soaked my low-hanging backside some time ago, and was now playing around my knees and elbows. My chin was only a couple of inches above my knees. What with the weight of water and the current, I wasn't sure that, if I fell over, I would be able to get up again.

I heard something heavy and metal being moved with great difficulty up ahead. I hoped the metal something was well above high tide level. If the hatch needed to be closed and dogged again to keep the water out it was going to be a close run thing.

The sound of screeching metal stopped. A flashlight played madly over the walls and down the tunnel for a moment. But I couldn't see anybody because they were – of course – standing behind the light. Or perhaps they were climbing up out of the tunnel.

I screamed, 'wait for me!' in case they felt they needed to close the hatch before I made it out. I tried to move faster, but I was all tangled up in the tidewater now. I moved slower, not faster.

The water was in my mouth and nose now if I didn't keep my head right back. As a result I couldn't see where I was going. I closed my eyes and stretched my arms out to the side to keep me upright and on course. Fortunately there wasn't much option about direction.

It was an excruciating way to travel.

But now hands caught hold of me under my arms and dragged me upwards. I bicycled my legs, hoping I'd reached the steps Freddie had whooped about, hoping to get some purchase on them. Gradually I rose from the waves. Carol said,

'He ain't no Botticelli's Venus is he?'

They all laughed. I tried to join in and started coughing.

They carried on lifting, and I began to rise in earnest. I could feel steps beneath me now. And here was a handrail.

'Right,' said Brandon, 'iron ladder behind you Andy – up you go. It's open at the top. Freddie's up there. He'll give you a hand.' Carol pushed me from below, her shoulder under my backside, until I popped through the open hatch into Freddie's waiting hands. He hauled me clear as quickly as he could pull and I could scramble, then turned to help Carol. I staggered a couple of paces and bent over, retching the seawater out of my lungs.

Carol popped up like a cork from a bottle of bubbly. But we had to reach in and grab Brandon, who emerged coughing and soaked through, but fortunately still clutching his mobile, the flashlight now a feeble glimmer. We looked at each other for a moment.

'Well,' I said. 'That was a stupid idea, wasn't it?'

We nodded. Carol said,

'Fun though. I've really worked up an appetite for lunch. What about you guys?'

Freddie and Brandon gave her a half-hearted

agreement. I managed a smile now that my heart rate was beginning to return to normal.

And, actually, when we thought about what might have happened, our deliverance was pretty sweet. A giggle started with Carol and worked its way around the rest of us. Soon we we guffawing with hysterical laughter.

As we hooted and cackled, my phone's flashlight gave out, leaving us completely in the dark, wherever we were. There was an odd, chemical smell – but it wasn't seawater, which was encouraging.

*

Then something quite odd happened: a light came on. We blinked owlishly, squinting to try and see what had happened.

A voice enquired, coldly,

'Who the hell are you, and what are you doing in our broom closet?'

Still squinting, we tried to get to our feet and move towards the light.

'O M G,' said another voice. 'They're soaking wet! And dripping all over the carpet.'

Carpet? My eyes were becoming accustomed to the light now. I looked around me. We were standing in a very small room. Around us were buckets and brooms, and assorted chemicals for cleaning things. In the open doorway stood a man in a suit and a woman in the universal black and white of hotel staff.

Freddie was rather less ebullient than usual as he

enquired where it was we had ended up.

'This is the Prince Frederick Hotel.'

'Whoa,' said Carol. 'Only the best for us!'

'Whoa,' I said. 'That's half a mile from where we started!'

'Where you started?' the suited man enquired.

'We went down a tunnel on the beach,' Freddie told him.

The woman said,

'They're drunk, Lionel!'

Lionel said,

'And it brought you here?'

'Yes,' I said. 'We were being chased by the incoming tide. We only just made it.'

'And what would you have done, if we hadn't heard you making a racket in the cupboard and got you out?' said Lionel.

'We keep it locked, you know,' said the woman primly.

'I guess we'd've sat here and dripped dry until the tide went out, then we'd've gone back down the tunnel,' Brandon said slowly and without enthusiasm.

I was wondering how, exactly, we would have dealt with the closed manhole cover at the other end. This broom cupboard had probably saved four lives today.

Brandon must've read my mind 'cos he added, 'Don't ever think of locking this hatch. Seriously. If anyone else was idiot enough to do what we've just done, they could easily drown without this way out.'

'And how many more idiots like you do you suppose there are in the world?' Lionel enquired sourly.

Carol grinned. 'Lots and lots,' she said. 'D'you have a public bar?'

The woman nodded, slowly and reluctantly.

Freddie said,

'You do realise this hotel is my namesake?'

'First round's on you then, mate!' said Brandon.

And we were off again, following our noses, in the direction of beer.

What lies beneath: 'like gnomes, with our knees banging on our chins ...'

Zeb's insurance

It was the dark of the moon, the night as black as the inside of a burlap bag.

The Fleet was unruffled; the tide had just finished coming in and was now at slack water before beginning to ebb.

Faintly the sound of muffled oars and exertion floated across the water. On the beach, a rock just above the high tide mark briefly unfolded itself, and flashed the light of a dark lantern, three times, towards the incoming rowboat.

In the little boat Joshua was suffering mightily. The dinghy he was rowing was heavily laden. His oilskins impeded movement and smelt both rubbery and fishy, which made Joshua feel queasy (and to regret the slab of greasy bacon in a bap which he'd consumed before setting out to keep his strength up).

The oilskins were not only a blasted nuisance, but also much too big, because Joshua had had to borrow them from the other occupant of the boat – a big man called Zeb. He was sitting in the stern, as he had done all the way, doing nothing but steering and exhorting Josh to row harder. Josh was certain he could row much better without the enormous oilskins getting in his way. Or even with a set of oilskins more his own size. But these of Zeb's had been thrust upon him, described as essential wear, before they'd set out rowing for the ship from Weymouth harbour at dusk. He felt like a pea in a tent, so he did. But Zeb was truculent as well as large, so Joshua said nothing and rowed on as well as he could.

His hands were by now a mess of blisters. He had decided early on that he wasn't cut out for this smuggling lark. It was nothing like as much fun as Zeb had made it seem last night in the pub. Perhaps, after all, he should go for a bank clerk with his Uncle Thomas, like his mother wanted him to.

At long last they nudged gently against the land, and Zeb got out and splashed ashore.

'Look alive, lad,' he said.

Josh shipped the oars as quickly as he could, but made an awful racket doing it. They were awkward to manoeuvre, being wound all about with rags to stop them squeaking. The rags were now soaked, and made the oars very heavy. No wonder it had been such a hard row in.

Finally he got them into the boat and himself half out of it.

In the distance lights bobbed. Men were coming.

At first Josh thought they were coming to unload the cargo, then someone shouted at them to stay where they were, and he realised these were the Excise Men.

A hand reached out to Josh.

'Hold this,' said Zeb's voice.

Then Zeb threw off his oilskins, quick as thought, and disappeared into the dark night.

After that Joshua could only hear the men coming closer and some heavy breathing and crunching across the seashore as Zeb legged it.

He was invisible almost at once.

But there on the shore stood Josh, holding the dinghy's painter in his hand, clad in the absurd oilskins, with one foot in the boat full of contraband and one on the shore.

There would be no bank clerking for Josh – not after being caught for a smuggler.

Zeb's insurance policy against being taken by the Revenue had worked very well indeed. For Zeb.

Zeb's insurance: 'Joshua's ... oilskins impeded movement ...'

The path to the moon

Rosemary and I had frequently holidayed together over the years. She was a good companion; uncomplaining, undemanding. Placid is the word I always associated with her.

This year we'd gone to Weymouth again. We both liked Weymouth. We'd booked a room high up in one of the tall thin guesthouses on Queen Charlotte Terrace.

The terrace was right on the Esplanade, with the beach just on the other side of the road. The view from our room was marvellous. The whole of the bay was laid out before us. We could see the people sunbathing on the beach, playing and swimming in the water, the children building sandcastles. We could see White Nothe at the end of the bay to the East and the squat, lowering presence of Nothe Fort on the West. At night the lights of the town lay round the edge of the great, sweeping, beach like a sparkling, jewelled necklace of many colours.

*

This one night, at bed-time, I came back from brushing my teeth to find Rosemary leaning on the windowsill, looking out to sea. The moon was full, and a rippling silver path came ashore on the beach right in front of our window. She said,

'Don't you sometimes wish you could just walk that path all the way to the horizon, and never have to come back?'

71

'Whoa!' I said. 'What's brought this on?'

'Oh, you know – mum. It was really difficult to find anyone to give her respite care so I could come away with you for a few days. And awfully expensive. And who knows whether they're treating mum nicely?' She drew in a shuddering sigh. 'Sometimes I just wish mum would die! There. I've said it.' She turned to me, suddenly fierce, and said, 'if I wanted to change nappies and purée meals and spoonfeed them to someone I would have had a child. I had offers!'

'I know you did,' I said soothingly.

'It's my own fault – I should've left home. If I'd once got away they'd never have made me go back.'

By the light of the moon I could see the tears running down her face.

'Why don't you sort out some long term residential care for her?' I suggested – not for the first time.

'It's so expensive. And I'd lose the house. I don't have anywhere else to live. Nor anything else to live on. The only income we have is my carer's allowance, mum's pension and her disability allowance. All together it doesn't add up to a pittance. If we had to pay rent, or a mortgage we'd starve. It's only that mum owns the house free and clear, that keeps us afloat.

'As soon as mum goes into a Home I lose the carer's allowance and the disability allowance. They offset mum's pension against the cost of her care, so that disappears too. And I don't get a pension of my own until I'm sixty six.'

'Are you sure you'd lose the house?'

She rounded on me.

'Of course I'm sure! Do you think I haven't gone into it? They *say* they don't take the house, but they *do*. They're *so* kind and understanding.' Her voice was hoarse with fury. 'They don't demand payment while she's alive, they wait until she's dead before they swoop. Mum wouldn't be cold in her coffin before they'd force the sale to pay her outstanding care costs. And let me assure you, there wouldn't be anything left. These care homes cost hundreds of pounds per *week*.

'They don't consider people like me. I'm supposed to be young enough to start a career. Ha! Nobody wants to employ somebody in their fifties. Especially if they have no relevant experience. All these years of caring for mum will count for nothing. All I'll have to show for it will be a basic pension, eventually. I have no skills except looking after sick, old people.'

'Couldn't you ...?'

'No I bloody well couldn't! It's bad enough looking after mum. I'm absolutely not going to look after anybody else's ancient, gaga, incontinent relatives.

'If I could even get mum *into* a Home that does 24-hour care, what would *I* do? And where would I *go* when I lost the house? What would I live on until my pension started when I get to be nearly 70? I've given up *everything* to look after mum. All she has is the house and what's in it. And what's in it is a load of old tat.'

She was crying in earnest now, great gulping sobs. I tried to comfort her, but she shook me off.

'I'm going down to the beach for a while,' she said. 'I don't want any company, thank you.' She pulled on her dressing gown, stuck her feet into her slippers and picked up the room key. 'Don't wait up.'

*

Poor Rosemary. She'd been stuck like this, between a rock and a hard place, for years. The private companies who provided 24-hour and end of life care had to recoup their expenses. Looking after people who had become too difficult even for devoted relatives *was* very expensive. I occasionally had a look around on the web, because of Rosemary's situation. The costs were frightening. £45,000 per year was quite modest. If nursing care was required as well as accommodation it could be a lot more.

I have always found the sea at night to be a great soother. I let Rosemary go and went to bed.

*

Some hours later I awoke with a start. For a moment I couldn't seem to catch my breath. I get like that sometimes at the seaside – all that lovely fresh, sea-laden air sometimes sticks in my throat. But I knew it wasn't that. Somehow I just knew.

I threw on my coat, stuck my feet in my Crocs, grabbed up my phone, and hurried over the road to the beach.

I didn't have to search very long before I found her dressing gown and slippers.

The path to the moon: 'crying in earnest now …'

Visitors to Lulworth cove

The year was 1588. Famous or infamous, depending on which side of the great sea battle in La Manche you were fighting.

The voyage up from Cadiz had been eventful enough for the Spanish, although confidence was high. Their new design of warship was almost twice the size of the English ships they expected to face. And they had more ships than the English, and on those ships, many more guns.

The June weather was warm, the wind a brisk breeze from the south west to drive them forward. God was, without doubt, on their side. The success of the invasion was a foregone conclusion. They had but to turn up to be victorious.

*

The ships of the English and their Dutch allies were small, carried less sail, and were much more manoeuvrable than the great galleons of the Spanish.

Between June and September the English and Dutch fleets harried the Spanish up and down La Manche and beyong, from the Bay of Biscay, along the southern Cornish, Devon and Dorset coasts, up and down past the isles of Portland and Wight, and along the coasts of Sussex, Kent, Suffolk, Norfolk and Flanders.

The English nipped and stung like a swarm of mosquitoes, then danced out of range of the swatting the Spanish tried to give them in return. The Dutch flyboats wreaked havoc in the shallow waters of the coastal North Sea, being able to slip in so close to the shore that they prevented the Spanish from embarking any of the troops they had waiting in Flanders to be ferried across, and which the Spanish needed to undertake the invasion of England once their armada had broken the English navy.

The English chivvying could be carried out under very little sail, which became another advantage when, in September, the weather broke and the sou'westerly breeze which had been so helpful to the Spanish at the beginning of their invasion of England in June became a gale, then a storm, and finally an act of God.

*

The big Spanish ships needed to carry a lot of canvas, which made tacking into the gathering storm to safe harbour on the northern coasts of France or Spain very difficult. It was easier to run before the gale, which they did – still pursued by the English fleet which saw them past Margate and into the North Sea, then turned back to find safe haven on its own southern coast.

In the North Sea, the Spanish stood out to sea and prayed hard. The worst was yet to come for many.

But not for the little corvette "La Cucaracha".

She abandoned her squadron as it was blown past the Isle of Wight and struck out on her own.

She answered her helm more biddably than the great galleons, which had to battle the gale with their noses and tails stuck high up out of the water. Under a mere handkerchief of sail, "La Cucaracha" turned successfully into the sea roads between the Isle of Wight and the mainland but, alarmed by beacon fires on shore and shots fired from shore batteries and beaches by enthusiastic English yeomanry, her Captain decided not to look for shelter there, but instead make for home.

"La Cucaracha" was tough, but she was taking on water from a long range cannon ball which had splintered some planking below her water line. Her captain expected every moment to be driven onto the vicious rocks that her lookouts spied on every hand. The south westerly gale that had become an Act of God still blew. Into its teeth the little corvette tacked back and forth along the English south coast, limping towards Spain.

Slowly but steadily, she made her way along, with short reach after short reach, for a day and a night, into the never-ending gale. Her leak grew more concerning: soon the pumps would be unable to cope. Her captain knew now that she could not get home without making repairs. They must find somewhere sheltered to beach her and do this. But where? Where?

On the third day the lookout spotted a tiny circular bay. Anxious scrutiny of the cove and the cliffs above showed no English cannon, soldiers, or yeomanry. The English had, apparently, gone home.

"La Cucaracha" didn't want to turn – she was

sluggish in the water now and listing badly, her bilges full of seawater. They coaxed her and bullied her and, finally, turned her. All aboard knew this was their last chance to save her and themselves.

The entrance to the bay was so narrow! Heart in his mouth, her captain took her in himself, his knuckles gripping white on the spokes of the wheel. The crew stood by with poles to fend her off the fiercesome rocks. A man with a lead line called out the depth of water beneath her keel.

And then suddenly they were inside the bay! Inside the weather was completely different – as quiet as if they had closed a door behind them. No storm touched them now: they floated, becalmed, in still water. It was like being in paradise.

The bay was almost a lagoon: the cliffs above them were white, the water beneath them turquoise. It could have been a Spanish cove. Surely that was a good omen?

They rowed "La Cucaracha" in, and beached her. Then they went ashore, for the first time in a week – staggering like drunkards after so long in such heavy seas. They went in search of food and water, dry clothes and shelter.

"La Cuchuraca" was as tough as her namesake. The captain had no doubt that they would make it home eventually.

Tomorrow they would begin repairs.

*

Note: of the 130 ships in the Spanish Armada of 1588, only 67 made it home.

Visitors to Lulworth cove: 'No storm touched them now ...'

A few words from a cox

The thing about gig racing is that it requires good teamwork. Without that the boat goes round in circles, or starts to rock and roll (and slow down), or the occupants of the little sea-going peapod end up black and blue from smacking each other with the handles of their oars. Take it from a cox, who knows.

An oar is a lever. The water is the fulcrum, the rowlock is the load, and the rower is the force. The work done by the rower must be balanced by the work done by the water. And in a boat rowed by more than one person the water must be working equally hard for each rower. That's not as complicated as it sounds, but it is the reason why a racing gig requires a cox.

The first thing you don't want among your rowers is an exhibitionist who pulls harder, or strokes faster than the other rowers, or – worse – does both at the same time. Rhythm is all: a harmonious rhythm is the thing to aim for. When a rower tells you that the others are slacking is the time you need to have a serious word in their ear and, if all else fails, ask them to leave the crew.

Alcohol is another no no. I remember the one time we rowed to Portland to celebrate a crew member's birthday with margueritas in 'The Boat That Rocks'. Ours certainly rocked on the way home. I called stroke: two oars pulled, one feathered, two doubled over giggling and one was quietly sick over the side.

Alcohol and physical exertion never go well together. We had a rower once who liked to bring a hip flask when we were competing. In the end I had to frisk her before races and confiscate it. It wasn't so much that she became unreliable – I could allow for her slight alcohol-induced lag with the stroke – but she would offer a warming swallow to the whole crew (even me) and no two of us reacted to the alcohol in quite the same way, making the cox's job impossible.

The cox's job is to make the gig's passage through the water as smooth as can be, to unify her crew and get them all pulling together. And when that happens, watch us speed across the bay! There is no finer feeling in the world than a harmonious gig crew. No effort, seemingly, is required: the oars dip and glide, dip and glide.

And the boat takes flight.

A few words from a cox: 'And the boat takes flight.'

The money pit

The hotel had a glorious façade. It stood, proudly alone, on the high ridge overlooking the bay, and gazed down with its many twinkling eyes on the holidaymakers frolicking on the beach below. Or it used to.

These days, rather a lot of the twinkling window glass was missing. And if you looked closely at the roof, quite a bit of that was missing too.

'A project,' Bil pronounced.

'A money pit!' Ben opined.

'Cheap,' said Bil.

'Falling down,' said Ben.

It was certainly a lot of house for the money. Considerably more than the guesthouse they had intended to acquire and run. Instead of, perhaps, five letting rooms this had twenty! To make it run would require the employment of staff in addition to themselves. And a lot of guests would have to want to stay in it, all year round, to make it profitable.

But Weymouth was a resort that never closed. Nominally a bucket and spade holiday destination, it also attracted walkers, those keen on water sports, and retired folk who came for that delightful and genteel activity 'taking the air'. Having drawn a deep, shuddering breath after the school holidays were over, from some arcane date in October Weymouth opened itself up to "Turkey and Tinsel" holidays, which delivered busloads of pensioners to the town. Could Bil and Ben grab themselves a slice of this year-round pie? Could the grand old hotel be made to pay her way again? Dare they give up their day jobs, and take this leap into the unknown?

*

First it would require gutting and refurbishing. (It had pretty much gutted itself already, as they discovered the first time they looked round it.)

From the ground (where a new damp proof course was essential) up to the roof (open-topped is never a selling point with a hotel room) their work was clearly cut out for them.

'It's only the same price we were going to spend on a guesthouse,' Bil wheedled.

'Yes, but that was for a going concern,' said Ben. 'Where is the money to fix it up supposed to come from?'

'The bank will provide,' said Bil. 'Leave that side of things to me.'

It was true, Ben mused, that his partner was a genius not only with figures, but also at charming blood from stones.

'It'd be cheaper to pull it down and start again,' said Ben.

'But it's so full of character!' said Bil.

'Woodworm is what it's full of,' said Ben.

Nevertheless, Bil persuaded him to come with her to see the bank about a loan. And enjoined him to leave the talking to her.

*

Ben thought the bank employee who interviewed them looked to be about twelve. Already her lips were permanently pursed from constantly picking holes in customers' business plans. This purveyor of loans examined them and their financial records with zeal. She seemed keen to prove that they were the mountebanks she clearly believed they must be. It was obvious she was as surprised as Ben that anyone should want to buy the pile of crumbling brick and rotting timber that the business plan related to (there were pictures). But Bil had prepared their case well. There was nothing in the budget for contingency (something the banker made much of) but everything else stacked up. And Bil had made the potential returns on the investment look positively mouthwatering.

*

Thus it was that, six weeks after first clapping eyes on the place, Ben found himself sandpapering the paint and varnish of many, many years off a seemingly never-ending staircase, while Bil stripped water-stained wallpaper off what she insisted on calling the ballroom. These were temporary jobs, while they sorted out tradespeople to come and replumb, rewire and reroof the place.

While the experts made the hotel weatherproof, Bil and Ben attended City & Guilds classes in how to plaster walls and ceilings, glaze windows, hang wallpaper, re-upholster, paint and lay carpet.

By the time winter rolled round the windows were, once more, twinkling over the beach below.

Bil and Ben had been camping in the dining room, but now felt confident enough of the new roof to move upstairs into the attic rooms under the eaves which would be their permanent quarters. The view was even better from up there: the whole bay was spread out before them. And as Bil pointed out, they would never need net curtains, up here in their own private eyrie.

*

Finally only the carpets and vinyls remained to be laid on the floors, and the curtains to make and hang. All the materials were on order. The kitchen was fully equipped, and they had placed their first ad for catering, housekeeping and waiting staff.

While they waited for it materials and staff to start arriving it felt as though their lives were on 'pause'. For the first time in almost a year the To Do list was in abeyance.

Bil spent these final days sitting at the prime table in the big bay window of the dining room with her laptop, working up their sales pitch and calculating costings, while Ben started to put the garden in order. Bil stopped what she was doing frequently, to look out over the sea. It pleased her immensely to think that shortly she would be responsible for helping others to enjoy this view, and the fresh air that came with it.

Ben passed her view, with the mower. She waved, he waved back. She gestured at the sea, he stopped the mower, turned and looked. Even he had a grin on his face most of the time now, she had noticed. Their mad project had come together better than even she had hoped. It was a dream situation. All they needed now was guests.

She drew in her breath sharply: there was something she had forgotten to do – they needed a name!

She waved energetically at Ben once more and threw open the sash window.

'We need a name,' she said.

He looked puzzled as he walked up to the window, and leaned his arms on the outside sill.

'For the hotel,' she added, mistaking his puzzlement.

His face split into a broad grin.

'Oh, she named herself ages ago. There's only one name she could possibly have,' he patted the window frame in front of him. 'I'm amazed you should even need to ask.'

'What is it, then?'

'There once was an ugly duckling ... ?'

'The Swan Hotel!'

The money pit: 'There once was an ugly duckling ...'

Where the gulls cry

Every spring, on the coast here, herring gulls come in from the sea to nest on our roofs and chimneys.

Throughout this annual enterprise the gulls are noisy neighbours; their joy, exhaustion and despair displayed loudly, at all hours, by both genders, and with infinite variety – something parents everywhere may understand.

During spring and early summer, as well as their usual cries (which resemble a crazed and over-burdened donkey sired by a banshee), the nesting gulls honk like seals, complain like sullen adolescents ('wha-aa-aat?'), express their frustrations with the primal scream of a solitary eagle patrolling the high sierra.

Their barnyard imitations are extraordinary too: they cluck and croon like happy hens, cock-a-doodle-do like roosters, whinny like horses, moo like mournful cows, bleat like sheep, bark like dogs, quack like ducks. But even such a farmyard of sounds is not the limit of their talents.

I have been woken in the early hours by gulls screaming like teething babies or yowling like fighting cats. They can to-whit and to-whoo like two owls at once. They wail like sirens, squeal like a puppy in pain or a kitten shut in.

They hoot like distant trains, screech like peacocks, whoop like gibbons from a distant rain forest.

They creak like a heavy gothic door swinging on

its oil-starved hinges through a dark and stormy night.

This constant cacophony bounces off the walls and alleys of the back-to-backs around me, through spring and summer, all day and all night long.

We get no other bird song.

Where the gulls cry: 'herring gulls come in from the sea to nest ...'

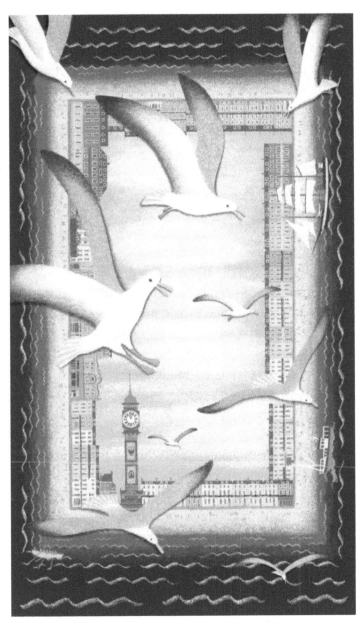

The mirror

She'd never been round the Tudor manor house before. She'd always intended to visit it. Previous near misses had been thwarted by weather, or inertia – then the house and most of the contents had been sold. But now it had re-opened and, before the novelty wore off, she determined to take the tour.

It was a fascinating house, the ground floor was resplendent in dark, ancient panelling, much of it carved. It was easier to see without the furniture. Fascinating. As the tour proceeded, she began to lag behind. Views from the heavily mullioned windows showed off the renovated gardens; a couple of huge pieces of Tudor furniture had been installed at key points; interesting doors with fancy red silk ropes across offered glimpses of narrow winding passages leading who knew where.

Here, for example, in an alcove in some sort of vestibule, was a particularly unusual mirror.

*

It was a long time since she'd looked in a mirror properly. Usually she just glanced at it when she combed her hair in the morning. There was nothing to be done about the face and body reflected back at her on those occasions. She was dumpy and plain. It had always been so and she had always known it. Not for her the rewards which accrued to the slender and beautiful. She acknowledged her own face in the mirror each morning with a raised eyebrow; it was just that same old face she had been born with: the face she was stuck with.

But this mirror invited her to step a little closer, to look a little deeper, past her attributes visible on the surface.

Or, perhaps it wasn't that it wanted her to look into it more closely. Perhaps …

She took a step back, startled by the sound of voices. The rest of the tour had returned from wherever they had got to. They flowed round her as if she was a fat little rock in a stream. Moments later the tour guide was extolling the provenance of a seventeenth century armoire in the room behind her.

She remained in front of the mirror. It was as tall as she, and wider. Its frame was a beautifully carved wooden frieze of forest leaves and fruits. A dark wood, walnut maybe. Not gilded. Not lit in its alcove, the moulding quite hard to make out. She peered harder and the moulding seemed to move, becoming slightly sinister. As she looked more closely at the intricately worked frame she began to see that the fruits were in fact faces among the leaves. The expressions on those faces were exquisitely carved and varied widely. Some seemed horrified, some struck with wonder, some puzzled, others beatifically happy. Here was a happy face. She ran her fingers down its cheek. It was warm. Wood was such a warm, sympathetic material.

Her fingers strayed from the wooden cheek across the surface of the mirror. And as they did so something strange, unexpected, wonderful happened – her hand went right through the silvered surface.

As the rest of her followed, like an egg slipping out of its shell, she realised she had one final choice to make before she became part of the frame of the mirror.

She began to smile.

The mirror: 'She began to smile.'

Miss Gertie Colhoun arrives in Weymouth

Miss Gertie Colhoun stepped off the train and looked about her with interest.

Weymouth was the end of the line (unless you were going to catch the boat train), so there was a real scrum to get hold of porters, luggage and children. Gertie could see at once that there was no chance of getting a porter. But she couldn't possibly move her trunk by herself. And even if she could get herself and her traps outside the station there wouldn't be any cabs, with all this gaggle of people in need of them. So, when they heaved her trunk out of the guard's van onto the platform she just sat on it and awaited developments. It was all rather a lark.

Gertie had never travelled anywhere much on her own, and absolutely nowhere by train before. The journey from Bristol had taken her most of the day. She'd had to stay awake all the time – despite the soporific snickety-snack of the train's wheels over the rails – to make sure she didn't miss her connections. And she was very glad she had – she wouldn't have wanted to miss *anything*. Her little stock of sixpences for tipping porters had been seriously depleted as she'd given them out freely to those who retrieved her trunk and wheeled it lugubriously around the stations, over bridges and through waiting rooms, to wherever the next train dozed, snoring and steamy.

She'd kept one last sixpence for this, her final destination. Although she would rather have spent it on a bun in the buffet car. But she was a sensible girl (if now a very hungry one). Otherwise her parents wouldn't have let her come away by herself like this. So now she was sitting on her trunk waiting for the rush to subside, pretending that she, Gertrude Mary Colhoun, did this sort of thing every day of her life and was quite, quite blasé about it, thank you.

But inside, her heart was pounding fit to beat the band. This was, by far, the most exciting day of her life!

*

The rush was subsiding now. She could see a porter with an empty sack barrow, and waved hopefully at him. He changed course in her direction. She got off her trunk, which the porter expertly upended and settled onto his trolley. She hung onto her Gladstone bag.

The porter set off for, she presumed, the exit so she followed him, hoping that she came across as a seasoned traveller, used to shifting herself and her luggage from place to place. Her mother had said that the world was full of unscrupulous people just waiting to take advantage of silly, naïve girls. Her father reckoned she'd be home in a week, broke or worse. But she wouldn't be. She just wouldn't! She made determined fists of her hands, in their cotton lace summer gloves. But their long artistic nails dug painfully into her palms, so she quickly stopped. And she could see now – there was the sign for the Exit. So she sashayed towards it as fast as she could, because the porter and her trunk were almost out of sight.

In reality she still couldn't quite believe that she had been engaged for the summer season variety show at The Pavilion in Weymouth town. Well, not just her. The lads as well. Between them they were Bristol Harmonics, a semi-professional trio of singers and pianist who had been in the right place at the right time for their act to be seen, and their services engaged for a glorious summer at the seaside. Arthur, the pianist, was going to play for some of the film shows too. And she and Ed were going to sing with the Melcombe Regis Big Band for tea dances, turn about. It was going to be jolly hard work. But here she was, in glorious Weymouth, without any portion of her family in tow. What bliss! What freedom!

Her mother had been beside herself at the very idea of Gertie going off to Weymouth and into show business until Gertie had told her how much she was getting paid,

'Two pounds six shillings a week, Ma! Including the tea dances.'

That was more than her mother got each week for the laundry she took in, and nearly as much as her father got at the shop. The money was a first rate argument in favour of Gertie signing the contract. (She'd already done so, but didn't tell her ma and pa that.)

But, the good money notwithstanding, her father had flat out refused to let her go.

'It'll ruin you!' he kept saying. Loud and soft, drunk and sober, he'd repeated that phrase over and over, ever since Gertie had been offered the job.

Yet here she was.

*

The lads were supposed to have arrived yesterday. She had hoped they might meet her at the station, but she couldn't see them. No. Wait. There they were! Trotting towards the station. Late, as ever!

Gertie skipped ahead of her porter and embraced the rest of the act enthusiastically. (Was it her imagination or did Arthur hug her a little tighter and longer than was quite seemly?)

'I'm so glad you've come. I didn't know how I wuz going to get me traps to the boarding house if you didn't.'

'Never fear,' said Bill. 'The other two-thirds of the 'Armonics is 'ere!'

In a trice the chaps had whipped the trunk off the porter's barrow as easy as if it had been full of feathers, hoisted it on their shoulders, and set off towards town. Or at least, Gertie presumed they were heading towards town. She realised she had no idea where anything was here (including their lodgings) and had better keep up.

But she remembered her manners, and first scrabbled in her Gladstone bag for that last sixpence, which she presented to the porter like the queen giving out Maundy money.

'Thank you, my good man,' she said, in her best stage accent.

Her trunk, high in the air now and swaying up the road above the heads of the crowd, was drawing amused (and some alarmed) glances from the throngs of people heading for the station and coming from it.

Gertie scampered up the road after the rest of the Harmonics, but couldn't resist a little free advertising,

'We're on at The Pavilion,' she called out to anyone listening. 'All summer. Come and see us, why doncha?'

Her father would've been mortified at her shouting in the street like that. Did she care? Not a jot. £2/6s a week! She could surely save something out of that. And if Arthur really was sweet on her, a whole summer together might be enough for him to propose. Wouldn't that be a lark?

Life really was just one adventure after another for a fashionable young woman in 1923.

Miss Gertie Calhoun arrives in Weymouth: 'Life really was just one adventure after another ...'

A price paid

There had been a fierce storm that week. When it had passed, Sarah put on her boots and her shawl, picked up her big basket, and went down to the beach to see what the storm had washed up. Sometimes goods off wrecks were washed in. There was often some coal, sometimes fish, sometimes nets or pots which she could mend and sell back to their original owners. It was a shame to profit off others' misfortune – but beggars couldn't be choosers.

As she trudged along the shingle, she could see the great sweep of Chesil beach all the way down to the next headland. There, she knew, the cliff hung over the beach, fragile and menacing. Today both cliff and beach would be golden in the weak sunshine. At this end the beach was greyer, always; the cobbles here were the size of a man's head. At the other end they were as tiny as pease. The sea roiled perpetually all along here, the undertow tossed the rocks about and sorted them according to size at the same time. It was a peculiarity of the beach.

*

Sarah had been hoping to find coal. Sometimes the tideline would be dense with it and she could fill her basket so full she could barely lug it home. Where the coal came from was a mystery. She didn't recall a collier ever coming to grief here or on the sharp off-shore rocks. Steamers used coal, of course, but only carried enough to get them where they were going. However, coal had been washing up on the Chesil ever since Sarah could remember. Her mother had sent her out after storms with a basket for sea coal when she was a child. Heavens, that must be fifty years! Her basket had been smaller then. Little else had changed.

*

It was early. Nobody else was about. She liked to be early, to get the best pickings. Although, if something truly special had washed in people always knew, somehow.

When a ship's cargo washed ashore it could lead to fights. There had been kegs of brandy beached once, before her time, which had set the whole village against itself for years. It was still spoken of sometimes, although relationships had been repaired. But it only took a careless word for the ill-feeling to start up again. Sarah considered that the sea's bounty was no bounty at all if it caused family, friends and neighbours to fall out over it.

The sea was absurdly calm now. But the sea was devious, and not prone to charity: it gave nothing for nothing. There was always a price to be paid for gifts from the sea.

Today there was no coal at all. The lack made her uneasy.

Tiny wavelets lapped at the steeply piled cobbles rising up from the waterline. We're all in tune with the sea here, thought Sarah, its good moods and its bad.

What was that, down the beach a-ways? Gulls were crowding round it. It might be a fish, perhaps still wholesome enough to eat.

She set off towards the excitement, the cobbles rolling and rumbling under her feet.

When she got closer she started flapping her shawl to frighten the gulls off, but they only walked a few steps and waited, regarding her with their cold yellow eyes as she stumbled up to them.

What was so interesting? What had the sea left for her this morning?

Oh. No. The sea gave no charity – for here was a man, wrapped in a seatangle of rope and weed and net, and several days dead. Most of his flesh was gone, but she recognised him by the remains of his gansey. It would've been unusual indeed had she not known the dead man. She remembered when her friend Eliza had knitted that gansey. Eliza had been big with child at the time, and unable to do much else. That was last spring.

Now she thought about it, she hadn't seen Robert in a week or more. She hadn't even heard that he was missing. Yet here he was. Not an unusual end for a fisherman. Not an unusual sight on Chesil beach.

Now she would have to traipse up to the police station for the constable. And then go on up to Eliza's. She hoped the constable would come with her. But she'd bet a hot supper that he wouldn't

She wished it had been coal on the beach.

106

A price paid: 'what was that, down the beach a-ways?'

The oldest house

It was the oldest house still standing in Weymouth and Gray was proud to be the current custodian of it (custodian: owner – same diff).

He'd loved this house since the first time he walked past it as a lad. All those weird angles to it; the tiny leaded mullions in the windows; the vast oak front door; the Portland stone trim round the mad, soaring porch, all carved by hand. He wondered what the back of the house was like, and its garden, behind the still sturdy brick wall which ran along the street – indeed, he drew imaginary versions of both, over and over, through his childhood. He had always wanted to own it: always had, in his dreams. Never thought he'd get the chance. Never thought he'd even get through the front door. Then he'd moved away and forgotten about it. But now – here he was.

He'd seen that it was up for auction. The picture online showed it had become very rundown, broken mullions, ivy getting in everywhere, the brick wall now sagging, ditto the roof. What could have caused its decay? Apparently the local wags had it that the place was haunted. How, they couldn't or wouldn't say. But it put off not just the flakey out-of-towners looking for a *pied à terre*, but also the locals wanting a fixer-upper. So the wags had done him a considerable favour. Instead of simply coming down to see what it sold for, he was able to bid for it and, heart in his mouth, acquire it.

Coincidentally, at the time he bought Chapelhay House, his marriage finally gave up the ghost. So there was nothing to stop him moving back to his home town and giving his dear old friend some TLC to bring it back into good order. He'd taken a series of miserable jobs to keep body and soul together and put all his savings into restoring his childhood obsession. This year he hoped finally to complete its restoration. Then he could open some of the rooms to the public in the summer and the house might finally defray some of his expenses on it.

When he first bought the house, he had traced the history of it right back to when it had been an inn. This hadn't been especially difficult, as the deeds of the property were all handed to him in a large tin box upon completion. The first deed in the box showed it as a going concern in 1643, known then as The Golden Grape in tribute to a notorious, recent local shipwreck. But it was older, even, than that. Tudor, definitely. The planking of the floors gave that away. He was still researching it in Dorchester's historical archive.

It was so easy to be led astray in one's reading. He found something about The Golden Grape, which led him to other shipwrecks, which got muddled up with local battles in the Civil War and then perhaps led him to the endless building and re-building of Nothe Fort just up the road. Never mind. There was no hurry. He'd lived away from Weymouth long enough. It had been time to come home. And what a home! Now he lived in *Old* Weymouth, where he'd always wanted to hang his hat, and soon his days of working for the man would be behind him. When he finally opened Chapelhay House to the public – with himself as a very knowledgeable guide – he could concentrate on his own little corner of The Naples of England to his heart's content.

*

After the plasterers finished in the withdrawing room, a lot of what they had used to imitate lime plaster of the period had ended up spread all over the floor by their boots. Gray started mopping it up as soon as they'd gone, before it went off. As he mopped, he noticed an absence of dust in the crevices of four planks in the middle of the room. He swished a little water round the edges of those planks, and watched it instantly disappear.

Very excited, Gray fetched an old knife from the kitchen and worked it gingerly around the dust-free joints in the flooring. He was on the fourth side, when the knife encountered some resistance and he heard a 'snick'. A section of planking a bit wider and longer than a coffin popped up about an inch proud of the rest of the floor, in much the same way that a car's bonnet opens.

He'd never known there was a secret door in the house.

Of course, it might just be a cellar. But in that case, why wasn't the entry point somewhere more useful, like the kitchen? And that hidden catch ...

More excited now than he could ever remember being since he'd bought this, his dream house, Gray pulled up the trap door.

Leading down into darkness was a steep flight of steps; narrow, with a handrail. It was likely that the steps – and handrail – hadn't been used in centuries. Gray was alone in the house. And just now he didn't want company until he worked out exactly what he'd found. So it would be wise not to fall down those steps and break a leg.

He fetched his phone, and the large torch which he had bought for the express purpose of peering up chimneys and into hidey holes and peculiar kitchen spaces.

Gingerly he reversed onto the ladder-like companionway and began to descend.

After the first six steps he had to relinquish his hold on the frame of the opening and trust to the steps and the handrail. Both felt solid enough. But Gray tried to be light on his feet as he descended.

*

On the way down he had stopped several times and played his flashlight around the walls he was passing as he went. They were stone. This was part of the foundations of the house, no doubt about it. A cellar, then.

He sniffed. No hint of damp in the air. Nor of any foodstuffs or alcohol either. Only dust. He sneezed. This was a very fine cellar.

At the bottom of the steps he turned and played his light around the room. Where the light didn't reach there was an oppressive sort of darkness. It felt ... heavy.

Was there a door connecting this room with the outside? Not that he could see. So the only way in or out of it was through that coffin-shaped hole. If the hole had been *upstairs* he would've assumed that it was, indeed, a coffin hole. But nobody would want to bring a coffin down here because of the difficulty of getting a body down here to lay out. Nor would you want to shift a body up from here either. The shape of the hole must be coincidental ... except here was something for which a coffin would've been very useful.

In the furthest corner from the steps a skeleton was slumped.

*

'Oh, my,' Gray said out loud.

Well, that explained why it felt oppressive down here.

Whoever the cadaver in the far corner had been, and however it had got here, it was going to do wonders for Gray's project of opening the house to the public.

His mind started working overtime. He got out his mobile and started taking photographs. Lots of photographs. To show where the body had been when he found it (because, obviously, it couldn't stay where it was). Then he pored over the bones to see if there was anything to tell him how the person had died. And when.

There were scraps of clothing – a little lace, a bit

of leather – but nothing to give him (a tyro in such matters) even a definitive gender for his skeleton.

Gray wondered for a moment if the body was, perhaps, modern? Were there any poppers, or zips, or anything of that kind? Nope.

He looked carefully to see if there was anything to tell him what the person had died of – a musket ball, cuts on the ribs, a severed hyoid bone (Gray watched all the American shows that were big into forensics – they jived well with his inquisitive nature).

Was there any rope? Had the body been tied up when alive?

But there was nothing conclusive at all.

This was irritating. Gray was happy to notify the authorities about his find – very happy indeed – but he was much less happy to have to hand over to them the investigation into how the skeleton had got into the cellar. The remains were Gray's ticket to a comfortable retirement. He had spent a number of years writing articles and papers about his house. But this ... He could get a good replica made and show it off to curious locals and holidaymakers alike. For a reasonable ticket price.

What was that? A rat presumably.

For a moment he could've sworn that the skeleton moved.

A little shudder went through him. He backed away towards the steep steps. He wasn't overly keen on rats. Perhaps he'd call that enough for today, see what he'd caught on his phone's camera, and get a couple of rat traps to put down tomorrow.

*

He was halfway up the steps, when the trap door slammed shut over his head.

At the same moment his torch went out and the screen of his mobile froze.

From the far side side of the cellar he could definitely hear rustling.

Liquidity

Florence walked through the warm fruity stink of the stableyard. Deserted of course. The last horse had left here twenty years or more ago.

A row of bridles hanging on the tack room wall jingled, making her jump. Something was still here. Rats most likely. Or the wind. There was always a wind out here on The Fleet. Not a breeze, more enthusiastic than that. Something to carry away grief and blow in hope.

Auntie Flo's funeral had been brief. Florence had been the only mourner. Auntie Flo had left strict instructions about her funeral, and Florence had carried them out to the letter. She had been alert throughout proceedings for anything unusual about the service, the committal. But she was pretty sure there had been no clues there.

To shake off the gloom of the service and subsequent burial, Florence took herself to the pub next door to the church and had a large, restorative single malt. She raised the glass in silent toast to Auntie Flo and drank half of the spirit in one go.

As it passed down her throat, making her shudder, she remembered something Flo had said to her once when they had been out for lunch together. Florence had had a glass of wine, and offered one to her aunt,

'I only ever touched alcohol once, dear. Never again. Once was enough for me. I leave all that to the others now.'

Florence knocked back the rest of her whisky, took her glass back to the bar and, with a wan smile at the landlord, left to go back to the house.

*

From the stableyard, Florence made her way up the cracked and overgrown path to the house.

Rawlings House was an enormous, untidy sprawl. Every time their ship had come in (often literally) the Rawlings family had built another wing onto it. But Florence believed they hadn't sunk all their fortune into it. Auntie Flo had been firm about that, back before her wits had become fuddled. Flo had told Florence – her favourite descendant and named for her – that actual treasure still existed in the Rawlings family, despite appearances. It consisted of payment made in jewels and gold by French aristocrats to Flo's smuggler ancestors for passage across the Channel during the Years of Terror (if you were an aristocrat) otherwise known as the French Revolution.

Auntie Flo had told the story of the treasure to Florence the last time the girl had spent her summer holiday from school here. Flo had been firm that she had actually touched this stash of treasure, as a child; that she knew where it was. Florence wished fervently now that she had visited more often after that. Had pressed the old lady to tell her exactly where the hoard was hidden. But the house became more and more dilapidated as the years passed: the dogs died and the ponies were sold. Florence grew up and lost interest in those sorts of things and started working for her living. Then suddenly, as it seemed, the opportunity had gone because Flo ceased to be able to look after herself, or recognise her beloved great-niece when she visited, and had been carted off to a nursing home. Questions like 'where is the family fortune hidden, auntie?' simply confused her. So the secret had died with her.

Florence had debts to pay off, and her creditors were not patient people. So she was extremely motivated to find where great aunt Flo had stashed the ancestral proceeds from those illicit trips to and from the continent.

She needed that stash.

*

Auntie Flo's solicitor had already told her that she was the only legatee. She, Florence, was the only surviving descendant. If she could find the treasure it would all be hers!

She disinterred the big iron key from under the planter beside the porch, unlocked the heavy wooden front door and pushed it open. Then she stood in the vestibule for a moment. The smell of damp was overwhelming. It would have to be sold, of course. Although who would buy such a ruin? Some developer would snap it up for the land, she supposed. And pull the old house down, and stuff some gruesome block of rabbit hutches on the site. That should bring her enough to pay her debts, if she could stall her creditors long enough to sell the place. The thought made her even more sad than losing Auntie Flo. Soon it would be as if the Rawlings had never existed. She'd rather keep the place and make something of it if she could. But there was no help for any of that. Unless she could find the jewellery the French aristos had used to pay for their passage to England.

Right, she thought to herself. If I were a stash of eighteenth century jewellery and bullion, where would I be?

She closed her eyes and let her mind wander round the rambling house, mentally logging loose floorboards she knew about; remembering which walls weren't solid; racking her brains for cubby holes and ancient built-in cupboards. Her mind scampered up into the attics (three sets of interconnecting rooms, reached by three different staircases), and scoured every inch of each of those staircases for a suspiciously creaky tread. She worked her way mentally through each bedroom, paying particular attention to the one Auntie Flo had occupied all her life: first as her nursery, then playroom, finally converted into the master suite.

She could think of nothing that wasn't what it appeared to be. Nothing. She was going to have to go through the house room by room. That was a lot of rooms. The house was not an attractive proposition for an overnight stay – and she needed to be back at work tomorrow.

But her mind's eye showed her one more door. Always this door had been kept locked. Florence had never been allowed in there.

Fishing out of her bag the torch she had brought

for this very purpose, Florence approached the door to the cellars. Still locked. And no key.

Not in any mood for niceties, Florence tried a trick she'd seen on American cop shows: turned and kicked out at the door like a horse. Things behind her cracked and splintered, but held. She kicked again, higher this time, and the lock gave way. A waft of cold, stale air hit her, and she nearly fell backwards through the doorway. Turning she saw a flight of stairs leading down. Wouldn't do at all to fall down those!

She fumbled around at the stop of the stairs for a light switch, but when she found it and clicked it on the darkness remained total. Undaunted she switched on her torch and made her way gingerly down the creaky steps.

The cellar was enormous – it must run under the whole of the ground floor of the house. She quickly realised that this must've been one of the last building works the family undertook.

The space was full of racks, and the racks were full of bottles. Just dusty old wine bottles.

Florence went to the nearest rack and pulled out a bottle at random. It had obviously been there many years. She blew the dust off it and shone her torch on the label. It was port, apparently. She put it back.

She wandered on, into the stacks. The racks were numbered, but she couldn't work out what the numbers meant.

This rack seemed to be red wine. Deeper in was more port, more wine, and at the back she found some crates of whisky. Glenlivet. This had been bottled in the Sixties. She enjoyed a single malt herself, and knew a little about them. Fifty year old Glenlivet was expensive.

She worked her way back towards the cellar steps. This time, when she pulled out a random bottle of wine she had a look at the date on the label. Most of them had been bottled in the nineteen seventies, eighties or nineties. Certain years recurred, others weren't represented at all. The oldest wines seemed to be nearest the steps.

Under the stairs, her torch showed her an old desk. On the desk was a ledger. She opened it.

Every bottle was logged with the date of purchase, the year the alcohol within had been bottled, the price paid, the estimated optimum drinking years and the estimated sale price during that window.

Florence began to realise that this wasn't just a cellar full of old booze, forgotten and mouldering – there was order here, and method. Someone had maintained this cellar. Someone had collected all this hooch. Someone actively bought and sold the cellar's contents. Someone. Auntie Flo! The woman who had told her niece that she had touched alcohol once and not liked it – yet had bought and sold it for years.

Florence flicked back to the start of the ledger. Always neat, the ledger had been written by several different hands. She found a page where one tiny, neat script replaced a loose, florid one. The tiny script was familiar. It had written cards and letters to her for many years. The top of the page told her that this was when Auntie Flo had taken over custody of the wine cellar.

Thoughtfully Florence picked up the ledger and made her way up the stairs. At the top she wished that she hadn't kicked the door in. She would have to go to town and get a good padlock to make good the damage. What was in that cellar must be worth a fortune. The ledger that she was holding in her hand told the story.

It would certainly cover her debts. It might be enough to refurbish her ancestral home. When she'd got her creditors off her back, she might even come back here to live, make something of the place. She had options. It was a long time since she'd had those.

'Thank you, Auntie Flo,' she whispered as she locked the front door and pocketed the key.

Liquidity: 'worth a fortune.'

Fortune telling on The Fleet

Madame Zucchara was a summer fixture on the seafront. She alone was housed in a booth painted a sexy red and embellished with mystical signs: all the others were painted sea blue and covered with pictures of ice creams and burgers. She had insisted on her delightful, red, council-maintained booth when she'd agreed her first contract with Weymouth & Portland District Council back before the century had turned.

Madame had been telling the fortunes of holidaymakers for what felt like generations. To be frank, the work had palled. She had become a little unoriginal in her predictions. Too many unfulfilled promises of tall, dark handsome strangers and unexpected windfalls had seen her repeat business drop off sharply. If she wasn't careful she wouldn't make enough to pay the booth's rent to the council this year.

She needed a new challenge.

Somebody mentioned that the Moons who farmed down at the Fleet were going to put on a gymkhana. Nothing like this had been tried for nigh on fifty years. But as the number of horses in those remote acres overlooking the Chesil beach greatly outnumbered the people, it was certainly the ideal place for such a thing. A large number of children more or less in control of ponies was to be combined with a country fair – local arts and crafts, a falconry display, the building (and subsequent storming) of a mock castle, mediaeval weapons of war, wood turning, minstrels, costumed re-enactments, fire eaters, and locally produced food and drink. Why not a fortune teller?

With so much going on, thought Madame Zucchara, she would surely find her mojo again. It promised to be the most fun she'd had, professionally, in years.

She offered her services, which were quickly accepted. Could they supply her with a tent? (Her booth being council property and far from portable). Yes they could. What colour would she like? She thought for a moment and then asked for black. Dramatic. Mysterious. Sinister.

*

On the morning of the gymkhana, Madame arrived early with all the other stall holders and demonstrators. The two fields being used were already a mêlée of ponies, children and various other sorts of livestock; people erecting booths of more or less sturdy construction; people in costumes from various centuries, enticing smells of onions and roasting meats; and peculiar things being made out of wood with a large and very noisy chainsaw.

Madame's black tent stood waiting for her, and she began to enhance it with the blood red voile and mystical symbols which she had brought with her for the purpose. She had her usual small round

125

predictions table and fringed gypsy shawl to drape over it. The crystal ball which she'd found in a junk shop so many years ago, and which had pushed her into her present career, a folding chair, and an oil lamp to hang over the table.

Lamplight was essential. Especially in this black tent. Usually, even when it was daylight outside, it was too dark in her booth to see much (the booth having no windows). It was essential to be able to see the punter, and their money, and equally essential that the punter *not* be able to see clearly. The oil lamp also provided an ambience – the smell, the flicker. There was a slight taste of the fires of hell about it in the twenty-first century. Madame Zucchara occasionally reflected that in previous centuries hers would have been a most dangerous profession to be in. The whiff of hell, the ducking stool, a fiery end. But nothing like that was to be feared in the twenty first century – even with all these re-enactors milling about with pikes, swords and pitchforks.

By 10 a.m. the first pony classes were being held in the main ring in the other field, the day was warming up nicely, and Madame Zucchara had a pleasing queue developing outside her black tent.

But it is not said for nothing 'never work with children or animals'.

*

In between classes, what to do with the ponies and children to keep them out of mischief? Someone connected with the "Once a Knight is Enough" re-

126

enactment society had had the bright idea of giving the mounted kids lances with padded tips and letting them tilt at some spare dummies on poles. It was decided not to do this in the gymkhana field, because all the shouting and galloping might spook the competing ponies.

So they set the dummies up behind Madame Zucchara's tent. Nobody thought to inform her of this. Why would they? Her name was on the front of the tent, not the back. A blank wall of black canvas formed a backdrop to the tots' tilting.

Small ponies are as wilful and easily bored as their riders. However, their riders enjoy poking things with sticks, so catastrophe was averted for longer than one might have expected by their sheer lust for violence.

But eventually one pony shied away from the whirling target dummy, cannoning into others. In moments 'let's all take our turn at tilting' had turned into one of those games where it's all jolly good fun until someone loses an eye. Taking advantage of the mayhem a ferocious little girl called Fiona took the padding off her lance and, as her parents momentarily lost sight of her in the carnage, charged the line of dummies. The point of the lance stuck fast into one of them. Fiona had the lance tucked firmly under her arm in the best 'Ivanhoe' tradition. Child and lance came to an abrupt stop. The pony declined to stop but did swerve in a most agile manner, throwing Fiona into the air and then onward into the back wall of Madame Zucchara's tent which, thankfully, broke

Fiona's fall. The canvas ripped asunder with the impact and the small child – now bleeding and wailing – landed at the feet of a bemused couple who had come to ask Madame how they might save their marriage.

Madame had consulted the orb and the tea leaves and was in the middle of giving them her standard spiel in such cases, ie that the Forces of Destiny were indicating that a child might improve relations, when one arrived at their feet.

'Not this one, obviously,' said Madame. 'I think this one has broken its arm. For this one we need an ambulance. No, the Fates suggest you make one of your own.' Madame dialled the emergency services on her phone while delivering her advice to the bemused couple.

'What if our child turns out like that?' said the wife, aghast.

'That is the spitting image of your bloody mother as a girl,' said the husband, getting up to leave.

'My mother has never turned up unannounced covered in blood!' said the wife, following him.

'She turns up pissed out of her gourd often enough!' the husband's voice could be heard fading into the distance as the St John's Ambulance muscled their way in.

'Move along,' the special constables told Madame Zucchara's orderly queue. 'Nothing to see here.'

As her new clientele dispersed at the front Fiona's pony, now left to its own devices, shouldered its way through the hole in the back of

128

the black tent and, presuming them to be rather chewy hay, began munching on the fringes of the shawl which covered Madame's sexy little predictions table.

Perhaps mobile fortune telling wasn't all Madame had hoped. She would certainly appreciate her booth on the seafront more after this. But she had, at least, some new material to draw on. She might, for instance, reconsider recommending starting a baby to rocky marriages.

An interesting morning, all things considered – if not what she had expected which, for a fortune teller could be considered unfortunate ...

Fortune-telling on The Fleet: '... never work with children or animals.'

Just another pile of sand

Weymouth has *the* best sand for sculpting. It is fine and holds plenty of moisture. Within the southern English seaside atmosphere of warm moistness you can create huge, complex images limited only by your imagination and how big a pile of your raw material you can be bothered to assemble.

When the UK was still in the EU, Kostas Panandros came, circuitously, to Weymouth from Crete, to spend a season in the town doing bar work.

During that summer he found he wanted to stay in Weymouth permanently. (The attraction was a young woman called Caytee and her little boy, Clacton. Caytee wore very short shorts over leggings and could drink Kostas under the table. Clacton had a smile that was a sunny day all by itself.)

Before he could say anything to Caytee about maybe moving in together, Kostas needed a permanent job. He had a strong preference for self-employment. Bar work was OK. But he found he disliked working for other people. Back in Greece he had owned half a bar with his father, which was hard but rewarding work in the summer.

In the winter he had retreated to a chilly workshop and made clay bowls, vases and figurines in the ancient style to sell to tourists. This was the work he really enjoyed, and he was good at it too. They sold the pots and figures in the taverna in the summer. He enjoyed people admiring his work.

But then his father had taken ill. The last season with the taverna had been hard. Kostas had quickly realised that the bar was barely ticking over. His father's pension had been subsidising it. As soon as his father removed that support and he, Kostas, needed to pay a waiter, the business ceased to be profitable.

At the end of the season Kostas put up the shutters for good, before the bar ate all his savings. His clay work wouldn't keep him. His father was slowly fading. His two older brothers were building extra floors onto the family home for themselves and their wives. The family home was already bursting at the seams. Which meant there was plenty of family around to look after his ageing parents.

Kostas realised that this might be a good time to see something of the world.

A year or so later he ended up in London, with his savings almost gone.

He quickly discovered that London was much too frenetic for him. He temped for a couple of weeks in a local bar, but really wanted gainful employment somewhere quieter and cheaper, where he could replenish his savings.

As his experience was in catering, Kostas asked his landlady about quiet resorts on the south coast of Britain. She at once sang the praises of Weymouth (of which he had never heard before),

'I go every year. It's lovely there. Beautiful beach, lots of places to eat and drink. They have a funfair for the kids, and donkey rides. And marvellous icecream.'

That sounded more like it. Kostas got himself a one-way ticket from Waterloo to Weymouth.

*

Kostas was prepared to work very hard for Caytee and Clacton, but he wanted something to show for his labour: he wanted to start a business that could grow. Caytee didn't know it, but her Kostas was an ambitious and talented man.

Actually, Kostas didn't know it himself, yet.

Kostas was making sand pies for Clacton, on the beach one afternoon. The child was more interested in his fistful of soggy digestive biscuit than the sandcastle. And when Kostas went to fetch icecreams for them all, the toddler trampled Kostas' hard work.

Kostas returned to find his sandcastle was now just a pile of sand. Rather a large pile of sand, despite the trampling. Clacton declared that trampling sandcastles and eating ice creams were his two favourite things in the whole wide world and gave Kostas a happy, sticky, hug. So that was all right.

*

The afternoon wore on. Caytee and Clacton dozed in the shade.

That pile of sand reminded Kostas of something. Like Richard Dreyfuss in *Close Encounters of the Third Kind*, Kostas was driven to reveal what he saw in that sand pile.

He applied himself to it, at first almost casually, using Clacton's bucket and spade. As the afternoon wore on he became increasingly impressed at how the sand kept whatever shape he gave it, and began to work into the rough outline he had started with. It felt good to be sculpting again. He was surprised how much he had missed it.

In between slathering his girlfriend and her child with Factor 50 and moving the parasol to keep them in its shade, he began to bring out details with a plastic knife and fork he found in the sand. For the really fine detail at the end he used the tail of Caytee's volumiser comb. (He made sure he slipped that back into her bag before she woke up.)

Finally he sat back on his heels to look at what he'd done. In his mind's eye, he had seen a beautiful woman lying on her side in Clacton's pile of sand. And as he worked, he came to know who she was: she was something from the legends of his homeland. She was Calypso, the nymph of Ogygia who tempted Odysseus to stay with her for seven years, but could not overcome his yearning for home.

And there she was: a life-sized sea nymph, with long seaweedy tresses, and a sea shell bikini top. The bottom of the big pile of sand he had turned into a fishtail, covering Calypso's bottom half. She looked a little Greek, and a little like Caytee. Kostas had particularly enjoyed working on the sinuous fishtail.

By the time the slumbering ones awoke, Kostas had attracted quite a crowd. And his straw hat, which he had had surreptitiously nudged to the front of his sculpture, was half-full of coins – many of them pounds, he was pleased to note.

The sand sculptures in town were mainly permanent, he knew. Nobody worked on the beach, daily, any more.

By the time the summer season was over he could make a name for himself. And the little empire he craved would have begun to form.

As he helped Caytee pack up their beach encampment he was already considering what he would sculpt tomorrow, and the day after.

Of course, he would have to wait until Clacton was napping, otherwise his hard work would quickly become just another pile of sand.

Just another pile of sand: 'a life-sized sea nymph,'

Nathan Daniels' accidental war

The beacons were seen bursting into flame all along the south coast – a sight to stir the heart of any man with breath in his body. Presumably the Armada of the Spanish had finally been sighted. Time to singe the King of Spain's beard, then!

As the Weymouth beacon blazed up, already men were leaving their work, tumbling out of doors, pulling on their hats and coats, and making for the harbour or the shore defences.

*

Aboard The Golden Panther, Nathan Daniels left off his work on the ship's figurehead and looked up – first at the cliffs, each now glowing with fire as far east as Poole he reckoned, then at a throng of men clattering down Chapelhay towards the bridge connecting the two sides of the harbour.

The finishing touches to the great snarling cat on the ship's prow would have to wait. She looked good and fierce already he was pleased to note. Enough to scare the enemy without her having to fire a shot. He just hoped the wet paint he'd just applied to her great fangs with such care wouldn't get smudged.

His imagination – and his wood carving skills – made him a popular choice when local shipping needed a new figurehead or nameplate. It made a change from replacing rotten timbers and caulking that was his usual work as a ship's carpenter, and he always jumped at the chance to produce something less mundane.

Being no sailor, Nathan quickly gathered up his brushes and paints and made for the gangplank, so as to be out of the way when the crew showed up.

Too late.

The press of crewmen jostling over the gangplank, onto the ship forced him back into the ship's waist. All around him men were making ready to set sail.

Now here came the captain with four young men – two of them boys really – all looking mighty solemn, heads together.

Nathan caught some of the Captain's instructions,

'Matthew? Make a signal. See if we can have the pilot boat tow us out. It'll be quicker if we can.

'Thomas? Send a post to my wife to tell her we're under way. Be sure to send her my love – there may be no further opportunity to do so in this life. Ask her to send the same wishes to the families of you midshipmen and lieutenants.

'George – take a bearing from St John's spire and lay in a course for Lulworth. We'll be able to see what's what from there. Once we have sea room we'll navigate by dead reckoning – so look sharp with those charts I gave you, Harry lad. God's Speed to us all!'

So taken was Nathan with all this ship talk that he entirely missed the diminution of tramping feet coming on board, which would have been his moment to slip ashore. Had he been familiar with the noises of the ship, and not listening to the Captain's instructions, he would have heard a moment's silence before the rattle of the gangplank being drawn in, quickly followed by the men beginning to sing as they hauled up the anchor. It wasn't the first time Nathan's curiosity had got him into trouble.

He thought of his own wife. She was going to get a shock when she brought his lunch down to the harbourside and found every berth empty, Golden Panther and all, all gone to war.

As the captain turned away from the boys Nathan stepped into his path,

'Excuse me, sir, but I seem to be coming with you.'

'Who the devil are you, man?'

Nathan straightened up and tried to behave in as seamanly a manner as he could.

'I'm a painter, sir. Hired to repaint the figurehead, sir.'

The captain's eyes flickered towards the snarling wooden cat.

'You do good work. Have you finished it?'

'No, sir.'

'Well, we can't have you and your paint pots dangling from the cat's jaws today. We're off to war, man! Are you a sailor?'

'No, sir.'

'Oh dear. Well, report to the bo'sun there. The man with the red neckerchief. Tell him I said to give you lubber work. Keep your head down, and you'll be home as soon as we've whipped the damned Spaniards, eh?'

They had cleared the harbour now, and the ship began to buck and roll in the stiff sou'westerly breeze. Nathan began to stagger.

'Go on, man – before you fall overboard!'

Nathan gingerly made his way aft, his eyes on the trip hazards all over the deck.

'Keep your eyes on the horizon. You'll feel less sick,' the captain called after him

Seasickness! He hadn't even thought about that. He raised his head and sought the horizon as instructed. But what he saw caused his jaw to drop in astonishment.

There stood the curve of Weymouth Bay, like half the inside of a great bowl, the town arranged around it like a decorative rim. Nathan had never seen his home town from this aspect before. It was an entrancing sight. He itched to draw it, but even if he had had the leisure to do so, it wouldn't stay still. Up and down it went. And sometimes side to side.

Nathan had to pause in his search for the man with the red scarf while he threw up over the side. He muttered to himself, as he straightened up, *I hope these Spaniards be easily beaten and us home by suppertime.* But the thought of supper had him bending over the side again.

Nathan Daniels' accidental war: 'finishing touches to the great snarling cat ...'

One evening at 'Aura'

Early and late in the season, 'Aura' attracts a small, dedicated crowd most evenings. They sit and listen to the music, which is usually acoustic guitars overlaid with more or less tuneful singing, according to who's on.

But tonight was different. It was nearly midnight. The crowd was thick inside, packed out of the door, spilling into the street. I could hear the music from fifty yards away, cutting through the competing electric rock and pop from the neighbouring clubs: the wild call of a gypsy fiddle.

I often walk past here with my dog about this time of night. Part of the pleasure is in catching the last part of the final set of the night. One of the three clubs usually has something worth listening to. Tonight, like the rest of the crowd, I stopped and listened entranced as the fiddler played like a soul on fire. The dog finished his business with all the nearby lamp-posts and tugged on his lead to go, but I ignored him.

*

Finally the music ran down, the tunes became slower, became laments, became short encores, until at last even the most enthusiastic applause couldn't coax any more from the violin.

As I'd been able to see nothing (I'd been listening from across the road for half an hour) I was curious to see who had been making that marvellous music.

So I waited to see who would emerge carrying a violin case.

*

I waited for some time, and nearly missed the event in the end: a small mousy woman finally emerged, carrying the giveaway case. At once the crowd closed round her.

I had expected somebody flamboyant, with flashing eyes and – well, a presence. But if I hadn't seen the tool of her profession in her hand I would not have believed such music, nor such stamina, could have been contained in her tiny frame.

I slid closer to her through the crowd. She was being buffetted from all sides as she tried to get out of the bar. Everyone wanted to tell her how much they'd enjoyed her music, wanted a selfie, wanted to be part, for a moment, of what had just happened. As did I.

But in the end I thought she'd worked hard enough for one evening, and I just watched her go.

One evening at 'Aura': 'a small mousy woman finally emerged ...'

Never upset

the lobster men

The harbourside was deserted. It was that sleepy hour of the very early morning when the day is so new that even the birds have gone back to bed for ten minutes with a cup of tea.

But it was also the first day of the summer holidays, and Toby and Jake were keen to make the most of it.

'What shall we do first?' said Toby.

The boys had made a list the previous evening before going their separate ways to supper and bed. It was a cracking list and they were very proud of it, but they hadn't even started on ranking it.

Jake pulled the crumpled piece of paper out of his shorts' pocket and looked it up and down.

'The first thing on it is car wash,' he said.

'Well, we can't do that yet. It's too early. Nobody's up. What's next?'

*

Their overarching plan for the holidays was to make enough money to buy the skiff 'Wey Swan'. She had been for sale since the spring and the boys had fallen in love with her the moment they'd spied her lying forlornly in her winter bed of weeds with a handwritten "for sale" sign lying on her front thwart. She was old and heavy and crabbed, and in need of a great deal of TLC before she would be a proper boat again, so no-one else had shown any interest in buying her.

Her current owner, who knew of the boys' intentions towards Wey Swan and had a kind heart, was allowing them to use the little boat while they saved up enough to buy her.

'Let's take Swan out fishing,' said Jake. 'We can maybe sell the fish and put the money towards our Swan Fund.'

'The best thing for selling is lobster,' said Toby.

'I don't think the lobster men'll like it if we start pulling their lobsters out of the bay,' said Jake. 'But the Bluefish restaurant might buy mullet off us, if they're big enough. We wouldn't need to go far for them – there're usually shoals of big 'uns in the marina.'

'OK,' said Toby. 'But we'll need some bait.'

*

By the time they'd dug enough rag worms and snuck a heel of stale bread out of Toby's mum's kitchen to use as bait, the tide was nearly out.

'That's good timing,' said Jake. 'The tide'll carry us up into the marina. Less rowing.'

Swan was so warped that she didn't respond well to oars: steering her was an artform and progress tended to be of the zig-zag variety. One of the things the boys were saving up for was an outboard motor for her.

They loaded themselves, handlines, bait, oars and anchor into Wey Swan and cast off. Sure enough, they only had to scull out into the middle of the marina for the tide to catch hold of them and carry them up river into the marina, where the mullet also came in with the tide to feed. They dropped anchor and baited their smallest hooks (because mullet have ridiculously tiny mouths) with wriggly worms and bread pellets. Then they settled down to wait for the pernickety mullet to notice the wriggling and smell the bread.

*

They were patient lads, and after fishing for several hours they had several good sized mullet in the bottom of the boat. They were beginning to think about lunch when the sky – so bright and promising at dawn – began to turn as grey as a wolf. Within minutes the wind had picked up, and swung from sou'west to nor'west. It began to rain. Being summer, it was warm rain – but there sure was a lot of it.

Neither of the boys had dreamed they would need waterproofs on such a lovely morning, so they hadn't brought any. They were quickly soaked through. But they didn't have time to get cold.

Rummaging under the thwarts for something to bail the rainwater out of the boat with, they found they had forgotten not only their bailing bucket, but also their life vests.

Then they realised that Swan was dragging her anchor, under pressure from both the nor'westerly gale and the outgoing tide.

*

They could see a big muddy ribbon of river water in the middle of the channel and knew they were in trouble when Swan started to move towards it. The River Wey, which flowed through the marina to the sea, was now running much more strongly than usual. A lot of rain must already have fallen further upstream. So now the wind, the tide, and the river were all pushing them the same way: towards the open sea.

'We'd better row,' said Jake. 'An oar each. We'll make for the western slipway down at the dinghy park. We've got plenty of time to get her into slacker water and over to the bank. All we have to do is move her across the current. Pull in the anchor when I say.'

Jake got the oars in the rowlocks and gave Toby the word.

The anchor came up like a cork out of a bottle. The sudden and unexpected lack of resistance upended Toby, who knocked Jake into the scuppers as he fell. Jake lost his grip on the oars, which the current promptly stripped out of the rowlocks. The boys scrambled to get to the oars before they went overside, but they were too late.

Jake said,

'We oughta put rowlock tethers on our list of things for Swan.'

*

Now all they could do was watch the boats and the harbourside passing, faster and faster, as they headed for the harbour arm. The dinghy park and the safety of its slipway whizzed by, unreachable now.

'Watch where the mud is,' said Toby. 'That's where the current will take us. If it takes us close enough in, we can try throwing the anchor to catch on a pontoon or a ladder or something.'

But the muddy current kept well away from the harbour walls. And the anchor rope was too short to fling very far.

Helplessly the boys watched the last pilings of the harbour slide by as Wey Swan shot out into the bay with the wind, tide and current all driving her on.

*

Looking back longingly at the safety of the harbour, the boys almost missed the lobster boat bearing down on them, as it made its way in with its catch.

Carli Jane's crew was, fortunately, paying better attention. Her lookout blew the fishing boat's klaxon, making the two boys jump and alerting them to another problem. Carli Jane's helmsman obviously expected Swan to get out of the way, but the lads couldn't do that. So they waved frantically and shouted at the tops of their lungs.

Somebody on board Carli Jane finally got the message, and took avoiding action just in time. The prow of the fishing boat swung past, missing them by inches. Wey Swan almost took flight on the bow wave, and the boys had to grab for her gunwales to avoid going overboard. Carli Jane began to slow.

Soon the boys and the dinghy had been fished

out of the water, the boys wrapped in blankets and given mugs of hot sweet tea. But Jake just couldn't resist saying,

'I told you. It's always a good idea to stay on the right side of the lobster men.'

Toby watched Wey Swan slowly revolving from the forward davit (from which she was suspended, rather precariously, by the bow) and could only agree (silently).

He reflected how very lucky they had been to meet Carli Jane on her way into the harbour as Swan was making her unscheduled way out.

He was certainly going to be very, very nice to the lobster men from now on, in the hope that they not mention to Jake and Toby's parents nearly running Wey Swan down, and the boys' lack of oars, lifejackets and bailer. The lads would be grounded for the first week of their summer holiday if their parents learned they had been so feckless.

They would certainly be better prepared in future.

Perhaps the lobster men would like some fresh, fat, mullet?

Never upset the lobster men: 'they waved frantically and shouted ...'

Ol' Pete's plumbing

The rain was Biblical. It poured down for days on Weymouth town. People scurried to do their out-of-doors errands and chores swathed in boots and mackintoshes, clutching umbrellas which billowed before them like spinnaker sails.

This chronic rain was most unseasonal in June. Dear, flaming June: that reliable period of sunny, settled weather – how the British look forward to her arrival every year. But this year hitherto weather-tight roofs and windows sprang leaks; roads ran like rivers; fabric and paper became sodden. It felt like the end of days.

Ol' Pete, retired fisherman and local pundit, was renowned locally for his ability to predict weather. He would get what he called 'a feeling in me nethers'. The cause of Ol' Pete's sensations in his nether regions was never diagnosed. Nor, indeed, was the precise location of his 'nethers' ever identified. But whatever went on down there had proved reliable on many occasions through the years.

His advice began to be sought. But at Pete's insistence Mrs Pete fended off all callers. He slouched around the house, listless and miserable, and declared that he had no weather advice in him. Except to say that he saw no signs of the rain stopping.

So, to enquirers, Mrs Pete vouched for the fact that Pete's 'nethers' were certainly in weather mode. But that this time his usual prophecy was not (so far) forthcoming.

Pete went off his food and became dispirited. Mrs Pete clucked round him in a concerned fashion. The rain continued to fall.

Something had to give. But when?

*

Mrs Pete tried him on her usual stand-bys. First she gave him peppermint tea. No change. Next she tried chamomile tea. Nothing doing. She tried apple cider vinegar, ginger, fennel seed, baking soda, lemon water and liquorice root in turn. Ol' Pete's nethers did not improve. The rain got, if anything, worse. Mrs Pete said to him,

'It's vegetable soup and wholemeal bread for you, m'lad, until this clears up.'

'Not even a drop o' milk in me tea?'

Mrs Pete was highly suspicious of dairy in this sort of situation.

'No tea. We dassn't take the risk, Pete. We've tried all Nature's usual remedies. Even liquorice hasn't helped! Now we must trust to plenty of roughage over the long haul to set you right.'

'You don't think 'tis a lack o' beer what's doing it, love? Plenty o' roughage in Guinness.'

'I do not.'

Pete's nethers were usually more easily sorted out than this. Mrs Pete went through an extensive repertoire of foodstuffs, fetching home, through the continuing storm, all the foods she could think of, or Google, with a high fibre content.

However, Pete's nethers and the awful weather were more stubborn even than the man himself. No relief was granted to Pete, or the rain-sodden citizens of Weymouth.

What Mrs Pete put in front of Pete at mealtimes began to resemble the sort of thing one might give an ailing horse. Weetabix lubricated with water (Mrs Pete was still firm about not giving him any dairy) turned into a dreadful grey sludge. Even with a bit of honey on it, she had to admit it looked unappetising. That caused her to think of proper porridge. But the porridge she served him (without milk) could have been more profitably put to use pointing brickwork.

*

The days passed, and still Pete's condition did not improve, even with all that roughage. His remark about beer made Mrs Pete think harder about his liquid intake. So she tried him on Coca Cola, beer (against her better judgement) and finally (after another rummage on the internet) prune juice.

After the prune juice the sun finally peeped through the clouds and the rain clouds blew off to bother Bournemouth for a bit.

'Thank goodness for that,' said Mrs Pete to her patient when, after a lengthy sojourn in the downstairs loo, he passed her on his way back to his usual chair in front of the TV in the lounge.

But she was speaking to an empty armchair – Pete and his weather predicting equipment had passed his comfy chair and were heading for the kitchen, appetite fully restored and intent on raiding the fridge for the good stuff.

Ol' Pete's plumbing: 'something had to give. But when?'

156

Dancing in the dark

It was just about midnight. A girl ran out of 'Zowie!' nightclub, across the road, and the Esplanade, and onto the beach. She was dressed for partying.

It had been so hot inside, she'd had to get out. She'd left Darren on the dance floor. He was behaving like a bit of a wanker anyway, to be honest, wanting to smooch every number – even the fast ones – with his hands up her skirt and all over her arse.

It was cool on the beach. And quiet. She stopped to take off her pretty party sandals. A gentle, salty breeze caressed the back of her neck, and the sand was soft beneath her feet. *This* was where she wanted to dance, on her own, on the cool sand, to the music spilling out from the night club she had just left. Now she was dancing as *she* liked to dance.

She got tired of dancing with no-one to admire her moves, and sat on the decking of the nearest ice cream kiosk. She watched at the glittering wavelets tickle the sandy beach in the moonlight.

If Darren was any good he'd come after her, wouldn't he? They could walk on the sand and look up at the moon. It would be romantic.

Here he was!

Her stomach did a little flip flop. He seemed more attractive at a distance. She got up and waved to him.

The distance between them quickly evaporated.

Now he was beside her, breathing heavily. Sweating booze. No, it really wasn't an improvement. But she gave him every chance, pointed up at the night sky and said,

'Look at the moon!'

But he didn't.

He was staring at her in a way she didn't much like. He said,

'I didn't think you were up for this. But OK. I don't have anything, so I hope you're protected.'

Fleetingly she thought, "protected"? What?

Without another word, he was on her; he pinned her up against the ice cream kiosk, his mouth pressed over hers, his hands everywhere. While he was kissing her – was this really kissing, this sensation of being sucked dry by a pump? – he was dragging her behind the ice-cream shack. She could feel his erection throbbing hot on her thigh.

He pushed her up against the seaward wall of the shack and started rummaging around under her short skirt to hook her panties down.

'No!' she said. 'No, no, no!'

'Too late to change your mind now, you little prick tease. The train's a-comin'.' He worked his knees between hers and began to drag her panties down.

She started to wriggle and push at him. Once he got her panties round her knees she'd be hobbled, unable to escape. She needed to do something *now*. She got her right knee back inside his, and brought it up into his groin as hard as she could.

He expelled air and folded over against her, his

face between her breasts. She managed to step aside and let him tumble forward. His cheek hit the side of the ice-cream shack with an audible smack. He slithered down it, grazing his cheek as he went. His hands weren't interested in her now, they couldn't even arrest his fall – they were cupping his painful balls.

She looked around quickly for her shoes, but couldn't see them. She didn't know how long it took a bloke to recover from being kneed in the groin, so she ran as fast as she could back to the club, to find Gilly and Mary.

*

Gilly and Mary, and their boyfriends, were loud in their condemnation of Darren. But she could see they thought she was making too much fuss about it.

'Will you come with me to look for my shoes?' she asked the girls. But when they looked at their boyfriends first to see if that would be alright, she knew the answer.

A light came on in a dark corner of her mind. She realised some things would never be the same again.

She'd been fond of those shoes.

Dancing in the dark: 'She'd been fond of those shoes.'

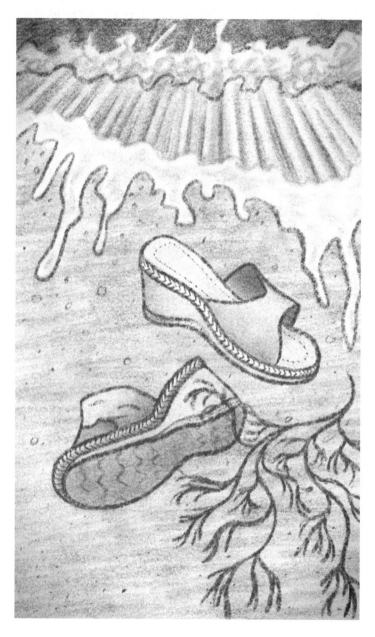

Motability birding

I was walking in Lodmoor bird reserve yesterday. I do this winter and summer, rain and shine. There is always something new to see. Even the over-sexed mallards and the Canada geese too lazy to migrate any more have their charms. That salt marsh really is a hub for birdlife. The pleasure is doubled when the weather is clement. Yesterday was a warm May day. If you wanted to buy a day like that, you could not afford it. My mood was as sunny as the day.

Not far into the reserve, opposite one of the viewing areas, parked tidily on the verge of the path, I could see some sort of wheeled vehicle a bit like a golf cart, with what looked like a tiny trailer attached. Both were painted in camouflage greens and browns. As bicycles weren't allowed in the park, forms of transport with more wheels than that certainly shouldn't be in here. My mood clouded over: I got ready to take umbrage.

As I got closer I could see, on the side of the path nearest the salt marsh, a substantial telescope on a large tripod. A woman of roly-poly build was sitting in one of those folding chairs that come in a bag, drawn up level with the telescope, with her eye to the eyepiece. She leaned back when she heard me coming,

'I'm not in your way, am I?' she called out cheerfully.

I could see right away that she was not your average birder. They are festooned with rucksacks, binoculars, woolly hats and insulated gloves, (even on a warm day like today) and wear cagoules and hiking boots. This woman wore an adorable plum-coloured felt toque, with flowers attached, jauntily over one ear. She was enveloped in a vast black woollen bouclé coat, from beneath which peeped black leggings. On her feet she had a pair of quality black trainers. She wore thin leather driving gloves on her hands – you remember the ones with the cut-outs on the back? They were also a deep plum. She was *smart* in a way that I had never seen a birdwatcher be before. My mood became curious.

Neither she nor what I could now see was a Motability scooter and an aluminium trailer, were in anyone's way.

'Not at all,' I replied truthfully. 'Can you see anything interesting?'

*

I have never yet met a birder who is not keen to share what they know, and what they're currently looking at, with a passing tyro.

'Oh yes,' she said. 'There's a marsh harrier up there.' She pointed. I looked along her arm and could at once see a large bird of prey, quartering the marsh. 'There's a little egret over there by those Canada geese'. She pointed again. 'And there are lots of swallows over the salt flats.' She made a sweeping gesture over the brackish marsh in front of us. 'They look like midges from here.' She smiled. 'I've got the big beastie trained on them just now. Would you like to look?' She gestured at the

162

telescope.

'I would. Thank you.'

'Let me give you some room.' She stood up and the chair-in-a-bag stuck to her bottom. She saw where my eyes were fixed, smiled and said, 'that usually happens. It's rather handy, actually – saves me having to work out where it is before I try and sit back down in it again. They're a bit rickety and I'm a bit big for them. But they're just the right height for the eye piece on the BB and they're easy to transport. I'm afraid you'll have to bend.'

Through the viewfinder I could see the acrobatics of the swallows with amazing clarity. 'Amazing,' I breathed.

'I know,' she said. 'I never tire of it. Just as well – I've invested a fortune in this rig.' She gestured at the scooter, the trailer and the telescope on its tripod. 'I'm a fairly static birdwatcher,' she gestured at herself. 'But I am loaded for bear, if there is ever one to be seen, which is unlikely.' She laughed and I joined in.

Just then I heard a strange bird call out on the marsh.

*

'Excuse me a moment,' she said, whipping a pair of Army grade binoculars out of the trailer and sweeping them back and forth to see what on the marsh was making the sound. 'Ah. Got him.'

I stepped back out of the way as she shuffled towards the telescope, with her eyes glued to the binoculars, yet careful to keep the legs of the

163

canvas chair (still stuck to her behind) clear of the ground. When she was in position, she began cranking the telescope to a new heading with one hand, while still training the binoculars on the object of her interest with the other.

'You're really good at this,' I said.

'Years of practice,' she muttered, working hard.

'Do you know what it is?'

'Some sort of godwit.' She'd got the telescope zeroed in now, and let the binos hang round her neck on their strap while she rummaged in her coat pockets until she found her smart phone. She held the phone's camera over the eyepiece of the telescope and took a picture. 'When I upload this picture to the app I've got it'll tell me whether it's black-tailed or bar-tailed. Don't you just love technology?'

I opened my mouth to say that I'd never seen a birdwatcher as well organised as she was, when she raised her head like a pointer.

*

'Do you hear that?' she said.

I did, now she'd pointed it out. There was a bird, far off, making a distinctive chittering sound.

'It's a Cetti's Warbler. Often heard, seldom seen. Possibly a pair, if I'm really lucky.'

Suddenly her little encampment was a hive of activity. In mere moments, the phone was stowed, the canvas chair dislodged from her posterior, squashed and dumped in the trailer, the binoculars swept into action, the flowers on her hat jiggled

164

merrily. She scrambled aboard her electric scooter and was already in motion when she said,

'If I can capture it,' she patted the pocket with the smart phone in it, 'I'll get in the club newsletter for sure!'

This was definitely my cue to get out of the way.

'Good luck,' I said as she shot off along the path, following the call of the elusive warbler.

Another day in the library

Priscilla De'Ath remembered very clearly when 'another day in the library' meant something quite different from what it did now.

It *used* to mean the place where her appalling family didn't bother her, where a welcoming fire crackled in the large grate, good editions of classic literature could be lifted down and browsed at will, her choice of her dead husband's secret stash of single malts was available at a moment's whim behind various of the false book fronts, and the key to this haven was always in her pocket.

The staff, such as it was, had strict instructions not to reveal her location. Higgins and Marta were to say, if pressed, only that she had gone for a walk.

'All day?' her son William would shout, exasperated. 'I need to talk to her about the accounts. When will she be back?'

And both Higgins and Marta would assure sir, very politely, that regrettably they couldn't say.

William Jnr was neither a reader nor a drinker. Two black marks against him. His ghastly wife, Sorayia (wasn't that a brand of malt loaf?) *was* a drinker, but only of Warrington vodka; *and* a reader, but only of *The Lady* and *Horse and Hound* and (secretly) *Hello!* She wouldn't have recognised a first edition of (say) *Gulliver's Travels* if it had been dropped on her head. Priscilla had been sorely tempted many times to try the experiment with an especially weighty edition resident in William Snr's library.

In the east wing (one of the least leaky parts of Todder Hall) had lived the excrescence which was her younger son, Alfred. He made up for the strait-lacedness of his older brother with wild excesses. If you couldn't glug it, snort it or inject it, it held no interest for him. The only good thing about his abuse of pretty much any substance capable of harming the human body was that it had nipped his sex addiction in, as it were, the bud.

*

She settled into her usual seat in this library, and booted up her phone. The free wifi was the main reason she came in here. That and the lift that carried her and her belongings to the mezzanine floor, where she could sit and watch the world of the library unfold around and below her.

The public library she sat in this morning was bustling, bright, warm, and sadly lacking in secret stashes of quality whiskies. There was nobody below stairs here whom she could ring to bring tea and sandwiches, the car round, or give today's menu to. If she tried it, whoever she asked would probably make a phone call to Social Services about her. That wasn't a problem. Priscilla had discovered in herself a gift for making up convincing-sounding names to give to busybodies.

And Priscilla De'Ath herself had been dead to the official world for over a year now.

*

168

Just another dead De'Ath. As dead as her beloved daughter. Oh, sweet Frieda.

Priscilla pulled the furred hood of her Barbour waxed parka up over her head to hide the tears. Of all the things she might have forgiven William Snr., her mad, stupid, feckless husband, drowning both himself and their lovely daughter in that boating accident was never going to be one of them.

It was, of course, inevitable that in-breeding on the scale that their two families had practised it down the centuries should lead to tragedy at some point.

Priscilla's side of the family was descended from Alfred the Great – hence the first name Alfred was bestowed on every second son. Tradition would have seen the firstborn daughter christened Aethelfrieda: both parents had baulked at saddling their sweet daughter with that, so Frieda she became. Down the De'Ath side of the family William was the traditional family forename, bestowed on every firstborn, for Guillaume the Bastard, better known to Norman Britain as William the Conqueror. Such bloodlines! As William Snr. always said, they should've been sitting in Buckingham Palace, not mouldering away in the country in a minor, crumbling stately home. There was a plot, he maintained, to keep him from his true inheritance.

Priscilla discovered too late that her new husband was barking mad. And given to wild assertions like,

'They'll be sorry, when I'm dead!'

169

They weren't of course.

At the time, there had been the police had enquired strenuously into the whereabouts of William Jnr. at the time of his father's 'accident'. But nothing could be proved. Nobody gave a toss what happened to the mad father of the family.

Although the whole family was devastated to lose Frieda. Which was everyone's best defence: nobody in the family would have murdered Pa if there was any danger whatsoever of Frieda dying alongside him.

After they'd buried him – a rancid day of veiled threats and backbiting – Priscilla had been puzzled to realise that she missed William Snr. Then she realised why: her husband was all that had protected her and her daughter from her sons.

And then there was the Entail.

*

The Entail had been the final straw.

Priscilla had been invited to the reading of William's Will 'as a courtesy'. Odd, she thought. But then, so much about her family was odd that if you ever successfully teased out all the odds and laid them end to end you'd have enough stuff to wrap Todder Hall in, much like Christo and Jean-Claude did the Reichstag.

But it turned out there was *nothing* for her in the Will. The Bloody Entail meant that the title and *everything* else went to William Jnr. Alfred got nothing. She got nothing. Frieda, had she lived, would've got the contents of his safe deposit box.

170

But as she had died with her father, that was subsumed back into the main legacy.

The solicitor said,

'Presumably you are happy for your mother and brother to continue living at Todder Hall, Sir William?'

There was a psychopathic glint in William Jnr's eye as he retorted,

'No bloody fear. Getting packing, you two. I want you out within the week. And don't think I shan't be checking your bags as you leave the premises. I want all the family jewels and silver accounted for, you thieving parasites.'

He really was his father's son, Priscilla reflected. What a pity. If only she could have proved otherwise, right about now.

Alfred moaned and wept and flopped about like a hooked fish for the next couple of days. You could sort of see where the propensity for burning cakes had come from. Then he did everyone a favour and drowned himself in the lake at the bottom of the ha-ha.

Fortunately, Priscilla was made of much sterner stuff, and had always been blessed with a fully functioning sense of self-preservation. She had squirreled a little away during the 30 years of her marriage to William Snr. It lay safe in a numbered bank account in Switzerland. Her sons knew nothing about it.

*

In the old stables out the back was an ancient

171

Volvo. The sort that tweedy women used to convey pedigree dogs to shows. Indeed, on reflection Priscilla recalled that the reason she had it was that she had won it, and a couple of Borzoi dogs, playing poker in some previous decade. She supposed she would need to find the keys to it. Ah. Here they were.

As William Jnr had made it clear that everything on the premises belonged to him now – including even her clothes, some of which he would be magnanimous enough to let her take with her – she had to move stealthily. As she laid her plans she felt much as she imagined Don Quixote must have done as he prepared his campaign to take a little evil out of the world. She was Donna Quixote and the Volvo was her Rosinante.

One thing was certain: she was leaving, and when she left, Todder Hall was going too. There had to be a reckoning. With luck, William Jnr would die in his bed this week. If not, at least Todder Hall would be reduced to a smouldering ruin.

The Hall's wiring was old. The timbers were rotten and infested with dry rot. The heavy wooden furniture and panelling were riddled with woodworm. Open fires were the only form of heating.

Who but the person who had kept this rats' nest functioning for the previous thirty years knew it like Priscilla knew it?

During the week's grace afforded her by her firstborn Priscilla ripped out wires, laid piles of kindling in unusual places, spilled petrol and sugar in unlit spots where nobody usually went, and bought half a dozen electronic firelighters.

She also got Bates, the gardener (who used to be the chauffeur when they still had the Rolls) to service the Volvo. She hoped she could count on his discretion, she said, as she pressed one of her favourite diamond and emerald bracelets into his hand. (He wouldn't find out it was paste until after she was gone.)

The night before William Jnr's deadline for her departure, she sat up reading until she heard him go to bed. She had packed what little she owned, and stowed it in the Volvo some hours before. She gave him an hour to settle down to sleep, then tiptoed around the house, systematically lighting her fires and locking the outside doors. Her carefully laid route took her, after setting the final blaze in the kitchen, to the back door. Twenty yards away her trusty Volvo waited. She pulled on her brand new camouflage bobble hat and stepped out of Todder Hall for the last time. She jiggled the car keys in the pocket of her brand new parka jacket.

In her other pocket she carried as many sets of the keys to Todder Hall as she had been able to find as she went round setting her fires. She was amazed at how many there were in bowls, on hooks, in drawers.

The staff all lived out. Higgins and Marta had keys. But this was not a precise science. Delay was all she needed. She was content to leave the fate of her relative to chance.

She pulled the back door to, and locked it. At

that point there was no further need for stealth, and she couldn't help but let out a whoop of joy. Then she scampered over to the old stables in her brand new hiking boots and slid into the driving seat of her trusty Rosinante. Bates had done a good job. Rosi started first time. As Priscilla pulled out of the stable block she was gratified to note the first rosy fingers of fire visible inside the Hall, through various windows.

As she drove away she threw one set of house keys after another out of the window. She felt more liberated with each toss.

*

She and Rosinante had made their way around Wiltshire, Hampshire, Somerset and much of Dorset before the old Volvo breathed its last some six months later in the park and ride at Weymouth.

Priscilla had become fond of – and good at – the nomadic life. But the loss of the car was a blow. She carried her tent and a number of mod cons in it. It also carried her entire wardrobe and leaked much less than the tent. Priscilla stayed with the dead car for two days, planning her next move, before repacking her traps and setting forth. For the past six months she had been a nomad. Now she would become a tramp. She had no idea what had happened at Todder Hall after she had left. She had studiously avoided the news for that very reason. The police might be keen to speak to her about it, or they might not. It might be assumed that she had perished in the fire. Or not. For the time being

174

she would remain in Weymouth. Perhaps until they towed the Volvo. Perhaps longer. Perhaps less long. It didn't matter. She wasn't on any kind of schedule. And the old car had no MoT, tax or insurance to lead back to her.

As she left the park and ride for the last time she casually liberated a Sainsbury's trolley and piled her things into it. Now she was a proper tramp. But the trolley was a bitch to push.

As she trundled past the Sue Ryder shop down the road she saw a large push chair for sale, and at once saw its advantages over the Sainsbury's trolley, made the purchase and then surreptitiously made the swap.

*

Currently she was wedged comfortably in the corner of one of the pale blue Victorian storm shelters on the Esplanade: the one next to Sand World. This was her favourite sleeping place. This particular shelter was set so close to the seaward edge of the prom that passers by could only walk behind it, not in front. The view out over the bay was unparalleled, and never obscured by the ugly terrace of council-owned beach huts during the summer. If she should pass a sleepless night, it was no hardship to watch the headlights of distant cars crawling over the headland to the east, the lights of the ships sheltering in the bay coming on at dusk and going off at dawn. And, as the bay faced south east, she had a good view of dawn itself from here.

As was her habit, she affixed a length of chain

around her waist and snaked it through the handles of the pushchair beside her. After all, it contained all her worldly goods. Except for her cash and her smart phone, which she kept down her bra.

One thing was certain, she liked the peace and the anonymity of her present way of life and was going to continue it. Occasionally she encashed a little money from her Swiss funds. Otherwise she slept rough, ate what she could scrounge and spent her days (and the rougher nights) thinking back over the her life. One day, perhaps, she might write her memoirs. But for now she'd continue her days in the library, and her nights on the Esplanade, watching the moon rise over Bowleaze, and the necklace of lights snugged elegantly round the edge of the bay.

She rummaged in her trusty Mothercare push chair and disinterred a bottle. One of the last of William Snr's single malts. Couldn't let them go up in flames.

A wee dram before sleep then.

Another day in the library: 'She wasn't on any kind of schedule.'

Crow

Crow sat on his usual rooftop. He could see the whole of Rickley Park from here: the row of aspens in which his relatives liked to pass their time, the thick hedges full of sparrows, the children coming and going to the two schools nearby, the people walking round and round with their dogs. He could watch his dinner fall from the hands of all those humans and pounce on it before any of the silly sparrows or his argumentative relatives realised something tasty had dropped. All the park's litter bins were visible from his well-chosen perch.

Last night there had been a fierce storm. It was that time in the spring when the weather was often wild. In the morning the other crows were squabbling even worse than usual because several of their roosts had blown away in the night and everyone was having to squash up. But nobody thought to join Crow on his roof, and that was just how he liked it.

*

When he turned his attention to the park, to see what tasty morsels the wind might have blown in, he saw something he'd never seen before.

He saw a silver bird.

The silver bird was perched on the edge of the nearest litter bin, peering inside with pale golden eyes. When it spied Crow staring, it looked him up and down, then opened its great golden beak, gave a hideous screech, and said,

'Orright, me an'sum?'

Crow blinked a couple of times. The silver bird with the golden eyes and beak was divinely beautiful.

The other bird continued,

'Cat got yer tongue?' and followed that remark with cackles of laughter. 'Geddit? Cat? Cat got ya?'

Crow wasn't sure if this was a regular bird, or some sort of angel. He thought angels would be more refined than this. He thought it as well to enquire,

'You're not from round here, are you?' he said.

'Nowr, bless yer 'eart. I'm from what we calls Weymuff. 'Tes on the coast, where all the salt water do lie, and a bliddy long way from 'ere, I can tell yer. But the weather's been so badly this past fortnight, and more of it to come they do say, that some of us decided we'd best fly inland for a week er two. So 'ere we be. Or rather, 'ere be I. Nobody else seems to 'ave made it yet.'

Very little of this explanation made sense to Crow, except the word 'weather', or was it 'heaven'?

'Are you from heaven?'

More cackling greeted this enquiry. The silver bird seemed to realise it wasn't getting through. It spoke again, ver-y slow-ly and loud-ly.

'Not heaven, no. Wey-muff. On the sarf coast.' As understanding had obviously still not dawned, the silver bird took a step back and asked, 'Whad-do 'ee think I am?'

But by this time Crow was able to understand

enough to reply,

'I don't know. I've never seen anything like you before.'

''Ee doan' get around much then, do 'ee?' said the silver bird, and commenced to cackling once more. 'Be a guided tour o' the bins in this 'ere park out o' the question?' it added, and winked its golden eye at him.

He was putty in its strange pink webbed claws.

*

When crow pulled his head out from under his wing the next morning, the other end of his roof and half the park was covered in silver birds.

A familiar cackle nearby told him which bird was his companion of the day before.

'The lads've turned up,' his silver bird said. 'It mus' be sprack 'n' spry down Weymuff still.' With that the bird launched itself off the roof and gave its mates the guided tour of the park's bins that Crow had given it the day before. Crow thought muscling in like this was a bit cheeky. He could hear the sparrows complaining. But there didn't seem to be much any of them could do about it. The silver birds now outnumbered the crows and the sparrows combined.

But when he'd watched the silver bird taking off, Crow felt a melting sensation in the general area of his loins at the grace and beauty of the thing in flight.

Bloody hell, he thought, I think I'm in love.

Crow didn't see the silver bird alone again for several days. The incomers were real hooligans. They threw the litter in the bins all over the grass so as to be able to pick through it more easily. They hustled the sandwiches and chips right out of the hands of the schoolchildren who came through the park. They didn't really roost when it went dark, but told each other ribald stories all night, cackling at their own jokes.

They seemed to be having a lot of sex, too.

When they were all together, Crow couldn't tell which silver bird was his. That upset him.

The weather seemed to echo his mood: it rained all day every day, and gales blew in one after another from the southwest. The sky was full of dark clouds, just like Crow's heart.

*

Finally one morning the wind dropped and the sun shone. As the day wore on, Crow noticed the silver birds were taking off one by one, heading southwest. If they were heading home, Crow was very glad to see them go.

Not so much as a 'thank you' for the bin lore, he thought. Bloody ingrates.

By lunchtime only one silver bird was left.

'I best be off,' it said. 'Might see 'ee agen, next time there be a big blow darn Weymuff way.'

Crow summoned all his courage (which was not much) and stuttered out,

'You could stay.'

181

'Nah,' said the other. 'This inland living's too tame fer I. I likes things a bit more lively. No offence.'

Crow thought that perhaps he did take exception to that. A crow's life was pretty lively. It involved a lot of rows with relatives, certainly. The old saw 'you can't spell "crow" without "row"' was very true. But then again, the silver birds were even more argumentative than his own extended family. And even bossier. And messier.

'I shall be glad to see *you*, any time you care to visit,' said Crow. 'But you don't need to bring the others with you.'

'Sherr, we likes to cleave togevver,' said the silver bird. 'A gull soon gets tired of its own comp'ny. But don'ee think I'm not grateful for the offer.' The bird winked at him out of its pale golden eye one last time then, quick as thought, darted out its head and pecked Crow on the breast with its great curved golden beak. 'Summat to remember me by,' it said. And with that it spread its wonderful silver wings and flew away.

Crow watched it swing round to the southwest and thought he had never seen anything so beautiful in his life.

*

The next spring, when he moulted, Crow noticed that he had a little heart-shaped patch of white feathers where the silver bird had pecked him.

That's what love looks like, right there, he thought happily every time he preened himself.

One of these days I'll fly down to the coast, and we'll have a high old time, me and my silver bird.

One of these days.

Crow: 'Are you from heaven?'

About the Author

I live with a variety of critturs, in a house like the Tardis, beside the seaside (where I do like to be). When I round the corner of my road on a blustery day I am forcibly reminded that I live less than 100 yards from the sea: result.

I am Cornish by birth, living in the county for most of my first 25 years. Thereafter, in the Seventies, I spent three years at uni in Aberystwyth. Then I found work in Milton Keynes.

I spent 17 years working for the Open University there, as a project manager; which was fun, varied and often exhausting work. In 1997 I left the university to write professionally.

Between 2006 and 2013 I returned to the Open University as a part-time Lecturer on their Creative Writing course, which was a tremendous experience and great fun.

Between 1997 and 2009 my short stories and poems wheedled their way into a number of anthologies and magazines.

In 2009 I published my first novel *Is death really necessary?*. I followed that with a novella *Little Mouse*, a volume of some of my short fiction, *Ice cold passion*, and released my second novel *Wonders will never cease* in 2017. Short extracts of these four books are provided on the following pages.

In 2016 I 'retired', whatever that means, and moved to coastal Dorset. Actually, I'm working harder than ever on delightfully diverse projects. There is glorious sea air and bucketfuls of fresh inspiration here, and I am loving it.

All my published work is available on paper from FeedARead, on paper and Kindle from Amazon worldwide.

If you have difficulty sourcing any writing of mine in which you may be interested, please let me know at judimoorea1@gmail.com and I will be delighted to fettle whatever you require.

Weymouth
May, 2022

Reviews are really important to indie authors like me. If you have enjoyed this book, can I ask you please to leave a review, or at least a star rating, on Amazon, or the website of wherever else you bought the book, or on my blog?

Thank you.

Extracts from my other published books

*

Wonders will never cease

1985

Thursday 3 December

The final Faculty Board of the year proceeded at its customary funereal pace. Fergus Girvan wriggled in his chair and wished its sagging, clammy plastic seat in hell – the moist warmth was playing merry murder with his piles.

Fergus and far too many other people were currently crammed into a single room in one of Ariel University's tatty, prefabricated buildings. Wan December daylight barely glimmered through plate glass windows already running with condensation.

1985 had been as dull as this meeting, for Fergus. For much of the rest of the country it had been perfectly bloody under the ruthless government of Margaret Thatcher. This year she had finally smashed the miners' into submission. Socialism was a dirty word. Greed was encouraged. The Welfare State was being dismantled. Public services fell by the wayside almost daily as their funding was slashed. Even at the university savings had had to be made. These were gloomy days indeed for anyone who'd ever voted Labour. And after seven vicious years there was no sign even of revolt from within the government. Thatcher cried 'on!' and the vegetables in her cabinet simply echoed her cry. Where and at what speed were questions they consistently failed to ask.

Now she had time on her hands Thatcher might well turn her attention to Ariel University. The Iron Lady hated anything Harold Wilson's government had put in place to make easier the lives of citizens not born into privileged families (never mind that she herself was a grocer's daughter). And Ariel was a soft enough target, being funded differently from conventional universities: it stood out from the crowd. It wasn't wise to stand anywhere the Leaderine's steely gaze could see you clearly. Yes, Thatcher's next quarry could well be Ariel. She might cut its funding until it ceased to be viable. Or she might try to snuff it out altogether.

Well, they'd just have to keep their union dues paid and man the barricades if the Gorgon's stony gaze were to swing their way next year. How bad could it really get? Surely in the civilised Eighties even the Mad Axewoman couldn't excise a whole university and get away with it? Looking ahead as far as Christmas, now less than a month away, was hard enough for Fergus. It was not his favourite time of year, not least because it was the one day when the pubs were shut in the evening. But at least the bloody phone didn't ring.

In an attempt to get something done while the meeting droned on, Fergus mentally worked his way through his diary for the rest of the year.

There was the faculty Christmas party yet to endure. That had historically been a ripe and ribald event, but more recently had become marred by limitations placed on duration of the festivities and the quantity of alcohol provided.

Some days before the Christmas party a meeting of the Architecture course committee was scheduled. Fergus was looking forward to that. He intended to present them with a pitch for a chapter on ancient architecture which would make their eyes water. He wanted to make one more visit to the British Library before giving Marion his draft outline for typing. It was yet another scintillating Girvan non pareil. Ground-breaking results from research into the sort of subjects covered by the term 'Classics' was difficult – the ground had been pored over so minutely by so many for so long. But Fergus had discovered something truly original about the Pharos of Alexandria in the bowels of the British Library and he couldn't wait to share it with his colleagues. The wonders of the ancient world had long been a favourite area of Fergus's study. Not so much was known about them as one might suppose. For instance, many scholars disputed the very existence of The Hanging Gardens of Babylon.

Which reminded him of a third professional duty remaining in the year. He was due to meet with a Hungarian PhD student who had a fascinating theory about those very hanging gardens: that they were, in fact, the hanging gardens of somewhere other than Babylon. This would explain much. And was certain to make for a fascinating thesis. He was looking forward very much to meeting Ms Jardanyi.

But as for the Faculty Board – all was, as usual, obfuscation and pettifogging. He didn't know why he bothered coming, except that people who didn't turn up tended to get lumbered, 'by a show of hands', with the faculty's shittier tasks. The last time there had been anything of interest to him on the agenda was when they'd agreed to fund his trip to Alexandria in the autumn. He permitted himself a smug little smirk. They would certainly find *that* had been money well spent.

Reliving the glories of an autumn spent in Alexandria, Fergus slumped into an almost pleasant torpor. As the lengthy business of recording apologies began, his mind finished revisiting Alexandria and segued into a replay of his fiftieth birthday celebration the night before. It began to rove pleasurably over the hills and valleys, some thickly wooded, of buxom Sukie, with whom he had spent that exhausting and rejuvenating night. What a quim – velvety as a mouse's ear and tight as ...

The sneeze caught Fergus by surprise, and his ears popped painfully. His body might be a temple, but recently it had begun to feel like a ruined one. He still hadn't been able completely to shift the sinus infection he'd picked up on the plane coming home from Alexandria the month before.

He glared at the window wall, running with condensation. What did the administration here think they were – guppies? This saturated atmosphere wasn't fit for human occupation. He could feel the bacteria which had taken up residence in his upper nasal cavities expanding gleefully with every minute he spent in this soupy air. The teasing pain in his backside wasn't improving his temper, either.

He wished he'd been able to stay in Alexandria for Christmas. His hotel had been comfortable, the food excellent, the weather balmy. The Corniche had been swarming with sophisticated young women. Of course, it being a Muslim country, alcohol wasn't too plentiful, but he'd managed.

The wearisome present intruded as the Professor of the Classics Department, Petra Stavrou, came in late and squeezed her way noisily past the massed knees of the faculty to reach a conspicuously vacant seat next to the Dean, Patrick Redman. Petra was always a top table person – all the department heads were – but she did not usually rate a seat so close to the godhead. Petra being his head of department, Fergus's curiosity was immediately piqued.

Petra was an ambitious woman, this reflected in her dress. Those fashionable padded shoulders, aggressively tailored suits, and gravity-defying stiletto court shoes were worn to show she meant business. She had joined the Classics Department several years after Fergus. Nevertheless, she had steamed past him in the promotion stakes, receiving the single, fiercely coveted, Professorship

available to the department two years before —
and becoming Fergus's boss in the process.

Petra was an able enough scholar, but
completely preoccupied with the location of the
texts and artefacts that were her specialism and the
staple of her study. She had a Greek mother but
had never lived in Greece. This combination of
circumstances made her, of course, obsessively
Greek. She had changed her surname to her
mother's patronymic by Deed Poll as soon as she
was old enough to do so. Greek artefacts should be
in Greece was her primary thesis. That so many of
them had been removed by the British, Petra felt as
a personal affront. Any and all campaigns for the
return of the Elgin marbles and similar collections
to their country of origin could be sure of her
support. About other areas of Classical study she
was rather less concerned which, thankfully, left
Fergus to get on with his own work unmolested
much of the time.

Why had Patrick placed Petra at his right hand
like this? Faculty politics was a deep stream, but
not a broad one. It took Fergus mere moments to
recall that a new Dean would be elected in the
New Year. It was Not Done to campaign openly —
one hoped to be *asked* to stand by one's peers —
but it did not do, either, to depend *entirely* on
reputation and respect. A little oiling of the wheels
was allowable, even expected. So, Petra had
ambitions in that direction did she? And, by the
look of it, Patrick's support.

In her absence the Department would require an
Acting Head. Ted was too old and Veronica was
due to go on maternity leave in the New Year.

There was no-one but himself! Fergus Girvan (Acting) Head of Classics. That had a nice ring to it. He could easily manage the extra work load – his current research project would be written up by the spring and his writing commitments too. He could see his way to helping her out. She had only to ask. He could hardly wait.

Fergus's career had been treading water for some time. His doctoral thesis on the Twelve Stages of the Hero's Journey had been an academic best seller. At his appointment in 1969 to the academic staff of the new, innovative, distance-teaching Ariel University (motto 'the university of the air') he had felt like a duck finding water for the first time. He and his new employers quickly discovered that he had a gift for creating course materials which could be taught at a distance. But his star did not rise. His Chair, which everyone considered a foregone conclusion when they hired him, had not materialised.

Not least because Petra snaffled it. She had worked out where in Greece a cache of very ancient marble statues had come from, and insisted they be disinterred from the bowels of the British Museum (where they had been mouldering for a couple of centuries) and repatriated. The Greek government had been effusive in their thanks and had established both a Research Fellowship and a bursary in the department as a result. After that coup her Chair was a foregone conclusion.

His only recourse was to submit a case for a personal Chair. He was particularly hopeful of success next year. He had ground-breaking research in the pipeline, nearing completion in fact, concerning his longstanding area of interest, the wonders of the ancient world. In addition, Ms Jardanyi's research, into the same area of study as his own looked very exciting. The result of his interview with her next week was surely a foregone conclusion. Her résumé was outstanding. To supervise her, surely exceptional, PhD would be a solid asset to his case. And now it looked as though he would be Acting Head of Department if – oh, let imagination reign – *when* Petra became Dean.

It looked as though his luck was finally about to change.

*

They nipped smartly through the agenda, penny pinching here, compromising there, until they got to the art historians' request for funding for a trip to Florence to help develop their forthcoming course on Renaissance sculpture.

At this point Patrick lumbered to his feet. The trip was being planned by Nick Bonetti, the senior Art History lecturer. Nick had obviously expected to be asked to introduce the item. He was trying now to catch Patrick's eye without having to put up his hand for attention like a boy who needs to leave the room. Patrick, on his feet rummaging around for his spectacles and shuffling notes, was resolutely not meeting Nick's eye.

Give him his bloody trip, thought Fergus, and let's get on. He glanced at his watch. The Vaults Bar would be open by now, and the bottle of half-decent burgundy which Chris, the Steward, uncorked for him on Faculty Board days for just this sort of eventuality would be breathing nicely. He could almost taste the first soothing glass.

Patrick was an imposing figure. Six foot three in his Hush Puppies, with a mane of silver hair and matching, luxuriant moustaches, he looked like some legendary ancient Celtic hero. His appearance, however, was deceptive. Patrick was more worrier than warrior, and these days used his considerable intellect to smooth the way for the government's frequent cuts to the university's budget. Instead of standing up for distance education, bloody banner raised, he did the work of the university's fiscal and administrative imps of darkness for them, arguing that a thrifty approach now would reap rewards when things got really tight. When Patrick thought the rainy day he was saving the faculty's pennies for was going to dawn Fergus couldn't imagine. It had been chucking it down in stair rods ever since Thatcher had become Prime Minister six years before. He had begun to fear that they would have to prise the doorknob of No 10 out of her cold, dead hand.

Patrick had got his glasses and notes in order at last, and was in full flow, setting the merits of the Renaissance Room at the Victoria and Albert Museum against the time and expense of actually going to Florence. The administrators were smiling and nodding, Nick was becoming apoplectic. The rest of his department (two girls and a boy) were whispering. None of them had expected this hatchet job.

Patrick ahem-ed his way to his coup de grâce. He said,

'So I don't see how we can support you in this, Nick – you see it just isn't ...'

Fergus sighed. It was time for action.

'If the Dean will indulge me? I have a few points to make.'

'*Must* you, Fergus? I really wasn't intending to open this up for debate. We still have a lot to get through ...'

He trailed off, in the pseudo-vague way he had cultivated over the years to turn wrath, and started shuffling papers again. Fergus was on his feet at once. Nobody told Fergus Girvan the matter wasn't for debate.

'I'm afraid I really must, Patrick.' Fergus whipped his own specs out of his top pocket and on to his face with a flourish, the better to watch the expressions on the faces of those present. His blunt common sense flooded the room, bringing balm to the souls of the beleaguered members of the Art History Department (pretty girls they were too). He unfurled his tattered and bloody banner, veteran of many a successful campaign, and spoke beneath it, straight to the heart and to the point. He said what needed to be said, neither more nor less, then he sat down.

Nick was right behind his standard,

'As Fergus has so ably pointed out, Patrick ...'

And it was clear the Florence trip was on.

Ice cold passion and other stories

*

The primrose way

'I had thought to let in some of all professions, that go the primrose way to the ever-lasting bonfire.'

(Shakespeare: Macbeth, Act II, Scene 3)

At the convent of St Nonna, Altarnun and Pelynt, Cornwall: May, 1972

They came to me as a deputation. They couldn't go on any longer, they said. It was too much for them.

'Perhaps we could borrow a rotovator,' Sister Kathleen said.

Sister Myrtle clucked her disapproval. 'No good. Never get it round the hedges. Have to have them all out. Months of work. Quite impractical.' Crisis always made her sharp.

'Perhaps ... a man, a strong man, just for the digging ...', Sister Iris suggested tentatively.

'And for the orchard.' Sister Cicely added. 'The tops need to come out of the trees this autumn and I've been wondering, Reverend Mother, just how we can ... the ladder isn't so good now and we ...'

She didn't go on. She didn't need to. I looked to Sister Adelaide. She could usually be relied upon to see a way through difficulty. Sister Adelaide said,

'A strong young man with no other calls on his time could soon get it in hand again. Yes, I think we need a gardener.'

They were silent, looking to me. I said,

'You realise what this means?'

Sister Adelaide nodded; the other three just looked at me, their eyes wide in their wrinkled faces and their gnarled hands fluttering about their rosaries. I sighed.

'I'll look into it,' I said.

*

It wasn't that we were unused to men about the place. Father Tyrone came to St Nonna's on a daily basis to say Mass and hear confessions; Mr Tyler the bank manager sometimes called – and was all too often in our thoughts; Mr Sanderson the milkman came whistling up our weedy path every morning, adding his strand of musicality to Prime; Mr Peebles the coalman came twice a month in winter; Dr Freeman called on an increasingly frequent basis. Men with a purpose, all – and a gardener would be no different. And yet the idea made me uneasy.

Perhaps my unease was caused by what our need for him meant.

We were getting older. Our last novice had taken her vows three years before. She had lasted a scant two more before she had come to me, her eyes swollen with weeping for her weakness, and begged to be returned to the world. We had never had a failure of that kind before. We were known as a reclusive Order, there were no late surprises for a novice to discover, nothing new to endure when the vows were taken. The withdrawal we brought to the novices was paced carefully. And in the modern world our seclusion could never now be total; we needed to interact with the community often, to buy our milk now we no longer kept a milch cow, to buy the foods we no longer grew, the clothes we no longer weaved and sewed ourselves.

I had prayed long and fervently to know what the Lord meant us to understand from poor Sister Joanna's abandonment of her vows, but had received no answer. None that I understood, anyway

And now: a gardener.

Later, as I watched my Sisters through my window, I reflected that it wasn't only the garden which was getting beyond us. The five of them moved low over the earth with their hoes, wimples whipping in the brisk spring breeze, tucked-up habits bunched around their calves. The window through which I watched had paint flaking from the frame inside and out. The gusts of wind which played with the Sisters' wimples reminded me of the slates which fell like leaves from the roof with every gale. Each was retrieved and tutted over, then joined its fellows, neatly stacked by the kitchen door. They made a goodly pile now. We put buckets and bowls in the attics to catch the rain when it came. Once we would have got out the roofing ladder and put them back ourselves. Now even all twelve of us couldn't get the ladder up onto the roof.

Everything here was past its prime.

I spoke to Father Tyrone about the problem of the garden after Mass the next day. He found the plan appropriate to our situation. Accordingly, I made yet another appointment to see Mr Tyler. He is a kind and realistic man. He promised to increase our overdraft facility to meet the need. Only after we had enjoyed a cup of tea together did he throw into the conversation,

'At least this will increase the value of your one and only asset, Reverend Mother. Anything you can do to look after the bricks and mortar – and grounds – of St Nonna's will reap benefits in the long run.' He looked at me over his tea cup in a way that made me think he had made a more sophisticated remark than I had understood.

On my way home I made a detour via the offices of our local newspaper and placed an advertisement – 'wanted: gardener, two days per week, payment by arrangement'.

*

He slipped into our lives, when he came, like a splinter under the skin does sometimes – you know it's there, but it's not particularly uncomfortable so you wait for it to work its way out again, and grow used to it in the process.

One morning there he was, hovering outside the kitchen door when Sister Margaret went out to retrieve our milk delivery for breakfast. It gave her a terrible fright. She came for me at once, having left him on the doorstep with Sister Elizabeth to watch him.

When I got there Sister Elizabeth was in the open doorway, holding a broom as if she was about to shoo a hen out of the scullery. The unaccustomed commotion had communicated itself to the others and all twelve sisters crowded behind me on the steps. He stood quietly before me – us – with a battered hat in one hand, feet planted squarely on the flags of the yard, back straight, arms strong, not young, not old.

Oh dear, I thought, what have we done?

Little mouse:
a novella

(Heroes come in many shades of grey)

PART 1: KRISTALLNACHT, BERLIN, 1938

Chapter 1

A tinkling sound woke him and drew him out of his
warm bed, despite the November night-chill, in
case there were fairies to be seen. Now he huddled
on the end of his bed peering through the curtain
and out of the window. The smoke of his breath
turned to ice on the glass; he scrubbed a hole in the
thin film with his fist wrapped in the too-long
sleeve of his pyjama top.

In the distance a harsh baying had begun. The
tinkling sound was getting louder and didn't sound
so musical any more.

Through the branches of the bare black tree
outside his window he could see a red glow over
the roof tops. *Something* was happening in the
next street. As he watched, a lick of bright flame
cleared the tops of the buildings and reached up
into the black of the sky. He drew back with a
gasp. But curiosity quickly brought him back to his

post. Dark figures were running ziggy-zaggy down the street. As they careered towards, and then past, his vantage point they smashed every window they could reach with stick or stone. His disappointment was complete: it was not fairy bells he had heard, it was these dark men in the street breaking all the glass.

He realised the street-lamps were all out.

He began to shiver. But he didn't want to get back into bed. Not yet. It was long past time for something good to happen: he had hoped this might be it. He could see a few figures running up his street. Above their heads bobbed flames on sticks.

He watched the people swishing their torches this way and that. Was this *Hanukkah? Hanukkah* was nearly a month away, surely? Mutti had been telling him all about it, saying that a big boy like he was now – he was nearly four years old – should know that not everybody celebrated Christmas. Some people had *Hanukkah* instead, and they were called Jews. One time, when Eva had come to play, she said that people like him weren't *allowed* to have Christmas – which seemed strange. And unkind. But she had flounced off to her mother Helga, before he could ask her what she meant. Helga was their maid and Eva was her daughter. He only got to play with Eva if she was off school, sick; or it was school holidays. Mutti didn't really like him to play with Eva. Nor did Helga. But he didn't mind it. She was six, so she knew lots of things he didn't.

But even at not-quite-four years old he knew that the *Hanukkah* torches should be in the

Temple, not out in the street. He liked *Hanukkah*. All the bigger children took turns to spin the *Dreidel* with the letters on it, and Mutti had told him that this year he would be allowed to join in for the first time. The letters on the old top were very important, Mutti said. They spelled out a sentence in Hebrew: 'a great miracle happened here'. The miracle had happened once upon a time, in a place far away from Berlin. Mutti had told him that they played the game with the *Dreidel* to remind the children that Jews only survived in the world against great odds. He was going to ask Mutti what 'odds' were, when she wasn't so irritable all the time.

Mutti and Vati were always short tempered recently. There had been a lot of whispering and sighing when they thought he couldn't hear. And conversations that went on late into the night, which sometimes included raised voices when they thought he was asleep. Vati never usually raised his voice. He was a man with a voice as soft as Mutti's silk blouses.

But recently they kept saying to him 'Theo, be quiet' and 'not now, Theo'. These days there was a hard edge to their voices that Theo didn't like a bit. Vati had spoken sharply to him this very evening, when he'd complained that his hot chocolate wasn't sweet enough. He hardly ever had any of his favourite things to eat and drink any more. The bread was always hard, nothing was ever sweet enough and milk tasted thin and sour – nor was there much of it.

Perhaps this of the torches was a special *Hanukkah* celebration to ask for another miracle?

And they had switched off the street lights to make it more special. That must be it. Theo watched the pretty lights reflect off the puddles of rainwater on the street. They poured water into bowls in the Temple to make the *Hanukkah* lights twinkle, too. Theo smiled and snuggled into the curtains to watch.

Suddenly a great crowd poured into the street, out of the alleys on both sides of it and up the road from the synagogue. They carried so many torches that the street was brightly lit by them – although it was an odd light; red and full of shadows. As the torches came closer he could see that they were carried by men, not children as they would be for *Hanukkah*. And the torches were great flaring dollops of fire at the ends of long poles.

Hanukkah lights were lovely, fairy things that fluttered in the least breath of air. These weren't *Hanukkah* lights. The men swished their poles through the air, and the fires made an angry, roaring noise. The men made an angry noise too. Their faces were distorted by the flickering fires they carried. Their mouths became big black holes in their faces. Bad words poured out of the black holes. Sometimes he thought he saw the red light shine on fangs in those gaping mouths. They looked like the bad wolves in stories. Theo became frightened: he curled himself further into the curtain, hiding now.

From downstairs he heard feet running, then Mutti's voice.

'Theodore – the synagogue. The synagogue is on fire!'

'Get the child. Quickly.'

His father's voice was barely raised, but there was something in it that the boy had never heard before.

Mutti came into his room too quickly for him to get back into bed. He turned to her to smile so that she wouldn't be cross with him not being asleep; but she gave a gasp with a scream in it when she saw him beside the window. She ran across the room, scooped him up and pulled the curtain back across the window properly. The room got very dark then, but Theo could still see the red flames playing on the other side of the curtains. Mutti held him tight in her arms, releasing her warm, lavender smell that always comforted him. He was always safe with Mutti, whatever bad things were outside.

Mutti went downstairs very fast with him clasped awkwardly across her chest. All the house was dark. Why was there no light? The house was always bright with light from the big windows, or from the electric if it was night-time.

At the bottom of the stairs Vati was waiting for them. He carried his walking stick with the silver dog on top.

'He was looking out of the window,' said Mutti. 'I don't think they could see him, but …'

'*HaShem!* – he could have done for us all. Quickly now …' He put one arm around Mutti to guide her, and with his other hand felt his way across the big, dark hall to the cellar door. He yanked it open.

'Hurry,' he said.

Is death really necessary?

1.1

On the 31st of January 2039 Teddy Goldstein left
Dunster castle on the Caithness coast for the first
time in two years. She was on her way to
Edinburgh to bury her father. Theo's death had
ended a father-daughter war which had
degenerated into endless campaigns of petty
spites and frustrations.

Teddy was wondering what she had left to live
for.

The jetpod ahead of them, carrying her
father's coffin, banked sharply as it entered city
airspace. Moments later their own jetpod
followed suit. Teddy glanced at the other two
passengers – her son and his partner, Rory. She
saw Ek give Rory's hand a squeeze as the jetpod
lurched extravagantly onto its new heading. Rory
was a nervous flyer, and the two loved to touch –
any excuse would do. The little incident made
Teddy smile wanly as she turned back to the
window. The huddled roofs of Edinburgh slid
beneath her, greasy-grey with rain. Edinburgh
was pretty in the snow, but it never got cold
enough to snow any more. Rain made the grey
slate, granite and encrustations of city pollution
that made up the façade of the city look
dejected.

Very suitable, then.

The jetpod continued to turn. The city continued to rush by beneath her. It made her feel queasy – but almost everything did these days.

The pilot straightened up, finally, and began to follow the railway lines into the city. The restored and Listed tenement blocks loomed up like cliffs in front of them. Teddy cursed the pilot under her breath. These flyboys were always ex-military, burned out by tours in Afghanistan or the Middle East and craved the old combat rush of adrenalin every time they flew. This one had saved his kamikaze tricks until now, so that the citizens of Edinburgh could hear him power up the boost and watch him make this dangerously steep and completely unnecessary climb. They swept over the old tenements with feet to spare, the blare of their own passage thrown back at them from the stonework. She tutted to herself: it had been a cheap trick and as a result of it she felt *really* queasy.

Now they swooped down over the elegant roofs of New Town, slick in the rain. January was always grey, and January in Edinburgh was one of the gloomiest places Teddy had ever known. She'd spent plenty of nights in underpasses, weeks in cardboard cities: she knew gloomy when she saw it.

It had taken nearly an hour to fly in from Dunster – which Teddy had discovered to be more than enough time for the sort of introspection inevitable when burying your father. Although Rory was the poor flyer, it was her Ek that looked the more miserable of the two. Teddy and her father had started badly and worked at making matters worse for as long as Teddy could remember. But Ek had loved his grandfather. Theo Goldstein was, after all, the only parent Ek had had when he was growing up. Today would be hard on him.

Teddy sighed. She owed Ek. There was a lot that he should know about his mother. But they had to get the old man in the ground before she could think about anything else. Besides, a noisy jetpod piloted by a burnout with a death wish was not the place for the sort of conversation that begins, 'there are some things I've been meaning to tell you'. And, fond as she was of Rory, the conversation she must have with her son was one that should only take place between blood kin.

*

The noise from the jetpod's engines rose to a scream and everything began to shake. The pilot had reversed thrust for landing. Teddy realised that even the fillings in her teeth were vibrating. Perhaps the train would have been a better bet, after all.

The noise and vibration got still worse and she lost her train of thought. Then she realised that, not only did she feel very sick indeed, she was now starting a brain-stabbing headache. *How appropriate*, her father would have said.

Theo had always been so vital. He had already been over a hundred years old when she returned to Dunster castle two years ago – and far fitter than she. He'd still been putting in sixteen hours a day at The Works then. Most of his veins and arteries were plastic by that time, his heart was plastic, as were his lungs, kidneys and liver – all developed by his beloved company and a boon to private medicine. But this year the little explosions in the blood vessels of his brain had begun and even Gold's Prosthetics had been unable to devise a way of reconnecting the delicate little blood vessels running through that particular organ. The life had gone out of him, week by week: the trips into the Works had become a struggle, then a chore, then impossible.

When the infarctions in his head had rendered him speechless she'd begun to go and see him every evening. He looked so tiny in the hospital bed, flattened by the bedding. Last night the only life in his room had been the tell-tales of the machinery monitoring his vital signs, beeping and winking with counterfeit cheerfulness. The old man in the bed had been waxy white. And now he was gone.

About an hour after she'd gone back to her own rooms the LEDs on the monitors had ceased to flash and the beeps changed to a constant wail. One of the identikit starched white nurses had come and told her, solemnly, that her father was dead.

Teddy hadn't known whether to laugh or cry.